**PAR**

Elizabeth Laird was born in New Zealand, when she was three the family moved to England. Since then she has travelled to the furthest corners of the world and has encountered all kinds of animals. On one adventure she became lost at night in a Kenyan game reserve, coming a little too close to an angry rhino and narrowly avoiding buffalo and elephants. Her experience of the wild animals of Africa has helped her write the *Wild Things* series.

She is the award-winning author of *Red Sky in the Morning*, *Kiss the Dust*, *Secret Friends* (shortlisted for the 1997 Carnegie Medal) and many other children's novels.

Elizabeth Laird has been helped in her research for *Wild Things* by Kenyan wildlife experts and ordinary country people, whose lives are constantly touched by the animals amongst which they live.

*Books available in the Wild Things series*

1. Leopard Trail
2. Baboon Rock
3. Elephant Thunder
4. Rhino Fire
5. Red Wolf
6. Zebra Storm
7. Parrot Rescue


*Coming soon*

8. Turtle Reef   April 2000


All Wild Things titles can be ordered at your
local bookshop or are available by post from
Book Service by Post (tel: 01624 675137).

## WILD THINGS

# PARROT RESCUE

## Elizabeth Laird

MACMILLAN CHILDREN'S BOOKS

*Series consultant: Dr Shirley Strum
with the support of Dr David Western, past
director of the Kenya Wildlife Service*

First published 2000 by Macmillan Children's Books
a division of Macmillan Publishers Limited
25 Eccleston Place, London SW1W 9NF
Basingstoke and Oxford
www.macmillan.co.uk

Associated companies throughout the world

ISBN 0 330 39301 4

1 3 5 7 9 8 6 4 2

A CIP catalogue record for this book is available from
the British Library.

Phototypeset by Intype London Ltd
Printed and bound in Great Britain by Mackays of Chatham plc, Kent

*For Sam and Rae*

*whose grandmother, Jane Fior, has been my editor through thick and thin. She encourages me when I don't think I can write another word, and always makes me do my best.*

# ACKNOWLEDGEMENTS

Macmillan Children's Books and Elizabeth Laird would like to thank Charles Mackay of the CITES Enforcement Team and Bob Wingate of the Animal Reception Centre at Heathrow Airport for their invaluable help and support during the writing of this book.

Above the green crowns of the giant forest trees, a flock of grey parrots wheeled in perfect unison. As if obeying a hidden signal, they landed together, settling around the rich harvest of fruits that lay, ripe and tempting, among the glossy green leaves. They began to feed.

One young bird, quicker than the rest, had eaten his fill while the others were still attacking the luscious fruits. He wiped his black beak on a branch to clean off the sticky flesh, then sidled further along the mossy surface to investigate an interesting crack in the bark. He began to tear at it, his sharp beak, strong as a wrench, ripping at the wood.

The young parrot paused. Far below, on the floor of this ancient forest, something strange was moving. He cocked his head, his yellow eyes, framed in a perfect arrangement of tiny white feathers, following every movement below. A thick branch, from which a lush fan of ferns sprouted, was obscuring his view. Moving cautiously, but impelled by irresistible curiosity, the young parrot shifted his mottled grey claws along the branch, sidling towards the trunk for a better view.

He could see clearly now. Two strange creatures were thrusting sticks topped with perches into the soft earth.

The other parrots had finished feeding now. They were fluttering about among the branches, squawking and whistling, making clicking and hooting noises, a whole feathered chorus, as each bird informed the others of its position in the tree. They were like a blossoming of grey flowers, their tails like brilliant scarlet stems.

The men had finished setting up the perches now. They had moved away, and the young parrot could no longer see them. He could see something else though. A feast of nuts and fruit was laid out on the perches, an array of the parrot's favourite food.

He hopped down to a lower branch, and looked more closely at the strange perches with their enticing banquet. Uncertainly, he fluffed out his feathers, stretched his wings then folded them again, opened his curved beak and with a soft hoot shut it again. He had never been afraid of danger on the ground. The enemy had always come from the clear blue sky above, out of which a hawk might suddenly fall, as deadly and swift as lightning, to snatch an unwary parrot away.

His curiosity was overcoming him now. Suddenly, he made up his mind, swooped down and landed on one of the perches. But as soon as his claws touched the wood, before he could even bend his head to peck at a nut, he became afraid. Something thick and sticky was holding him down. He tried to lift his claws, one after the other, out of the glue that had been smeared over the wood, but he couldn't free himself. He batted his wings and squawked in terror. Other parrots from his home flock had followed him now, and the perches were crowded with struggling, screeching, terrified birds.

Then, as the young parrot tried one last time to free himself, men rushed out from the surrounding undergrowth. Rough hands closed round him. He was caught.

# 1
# SUNNY

Tom walked out of his garden gate and turned left. He stopped beside the broken fence of the house next door. It had been painted green once, but now it was almost hidden under a riotous mixture of pink roses and purple bougainvillea that rambled unchecked, pinning open the broken gate, which clearly hadn't shut for years.

A strange sound was coming from behind the ramshackle bungalow, half-hidden under a thicket of trees. It was a squawky, whistling kind of noise.

Tom frowned. His friends, Afra and Joseph, lived here, but of all Afra's many pets, none had ever made a sound like that.

A tall African boy in a blue school uniform came out of a small house at the side of the bungalow. He looked up and saw Tom.

'*Jambo*, Tom!' he said, a friendly smile spreading over his face.

'What's making that noise?' said Tom, walking into the garden towards him. 'Is Afra at home?'

'Yes, she is. And did you know? She's got a parrot. Come and see.'

'A parrot? Wow!' said Tom enviously, following Joseph round the side of the bungalow.

'It's not hers,' said Joseph. 'Mrs Singh asked her to look after it while she's in India. Just for one week only.'

'Who's Mrs Singh?'

'You know. Afra says her daughter goes to your school. Jaswant.'

'Oh, Jas.' Tom frowned. 'I know her. She's older than me.'

They had come round the side of the house now. Beyond a stretch of neglected grass, a huge cage stood in the shelter of a magnificent old tree. Afra, a golden-skinned girl with a mop of dark curly hair, was sitting inside the cage on a log of wood. A brown goose was pecking anxiously around her feet, while clinging to her forefinger, his head bobbing nervously up and down, was a grey parrot. A small yellow-haired dog was running up and down excitedly outside the cage, giving vent to his feelings in a chorus of whines and sharp little barks.

Afra greeted Tom and Joseph with a gasp of relief.

'Thank goodness you came, you guys. I'm going crazy here. Sunny hasn't settled down at all. He's real nervous. He just took a big bite out of my thumb. And Stumpy's all upset because he doesn't like to have another bird in his cage. And look at Wusha! He keeps on barking and trying to get at Sunny. I guess he's wild with jealousy.'

'I'll take him into the house,' said Joseph, grabbing the little dog's collar and hauling him away.

'Thanks,' Afra called out after him gratefully.

'Do you want me to come in there with you and sort of play with Stumpy, to keep him off you?' said Tom, eyeing the parrot with wary fascination.

'Yes. Great.'

Afra moved her hand down to her knee, and the parrot sidled onto it. She winced as the sharp black tips of his claws dug through her thin cotton shorts into her leg.

'No, Sunny,' she crooned. 'That hurts.'

The parrot cocked his head and looked up at her with one bright black eye. Then he put his head down, begging to be stroked. Afra obliged, smoothing his lovely white-tinged head feathers with a sure, comforting touch.

Tom sat down on the log beside her, putting out his foot so that Stumpy, the goose, who loved shoes, could nibble at his laces.

'Does he talk?' he whispered.

'Yes, lots,' said Afra, in a normal voice. 'Only when he wants to, though.'

Sunny pulled his head out from under Afra's hand and regarded Tom with a steady eye. He seemed to be thinking. Then he fluffed out his neck and head feathers and spread out his tail, showing off a flash of brilliant flame-coloured feathers.

'Watch out,' said Afra. 'He gets mad with people sometimes. He's real moody, Mrs Singh says.'

'Why did she let you have him? Why isn't Jas looking after him?'

'She can't. Her class have gone on a field trip, don't you remember? And Sunny likes me. He talks to me for hours whenever I go to see him, so Mrs Singh reckoned he'd do OK with me. I guess I'm bird-sitting for her.'

'Does he really talk?' said Tom, who had only heard one word in Afra's whole speech. 'What does he say?'

'Oh, you know. Parrot talk, mostly. Whistles and squawks and things like that. But he does really weird imitations too, like the telephone ringing. He drove Prof mad yesterday because he kept doing his telephone noise, and Prof kept rushing to answer it.'

She laughed. Tom tried to imagine Professor Tovey, Afra's father, being driven mad, and easily succeeded.

'Sunny's even started to bark like Wusha,' Afra went on. 'That's what he was doing when you came. It drove poor old Wusha crazy.'

'But what about actual words?' said Tom. 'You know – Hello Polly, and stuff like that?'

'Words? Oh sure. Watch this.' She put her

finger down again, and when Sunny had clambered onto it, lifted him to her face. 'Hi, Sunny,' she said. 'How are you?'

Tom held his breath.

'I'm fine,' Sunny said, in a clear, rasping voice. 'How are you?'

'I'm fine, too,' said Afra.

'Wow!' Tom's voice was filled with awe. 'That's so amazing. Do you reckon he'd do it with me?'

Afra shrugged.

'I don't know. Try.'

Tom cleared his throat.

'Hi, Sunny,' he said.

The parrot looked at him, and bobbed his head up and down. Then he looked back at Afra.

'Wanna nut,' he said.

'No, no nuts. Tom's talking to you,' she said sternly, as if she was speaking to a child.

Tom stared at her in amazement.

'It's like he really understands,' he said. 'Like he really talks, I mean. Knows what he's saying and everything.'

She shook her head.

'Mrs Singh says he doesn't really.' She put her hand down on the log. Sunny stepped off her finger, then hopped to the ground, alarming Stumpy, who seemed about to hiss, but thought better of it. 'It's not like human language. I mean, they have their own kind of communication with each other in the forest, calls that mean things,

8

like "danger" and stuff like that. And you can train them to connect words with things, like get them to say hi to people they know, or say something that makes a person give them food. It's more as if they get into the habit of making sounds in the right places, you know, copying things that go together, like saying "Come in," when the doorbell rings. Sunny does that. It makes me crack up.'

'He's just so clever,' said Tom respectfully. 'I had no idea.'

'Clever? He's brilliant! They did some intelligence tests on parrots, some scientists did, I mean – the same tests they give dolphins. You know how brainy dolphins are? Well, get this. The parrots came out even better than the dolphins.'

Sunny had been walking sideways along the log towards Tom. He stopped, lowered his beak, and nibbled at the bottom of Tom's shirt. Tom suppressed a gasp. Then, slowly and deliberately, Sunny hopped onto Tom's knee and began to climb up his chest, digging his claws into the thick cotton of Tom's shirt and using his beak for leverage at the same time. Excitement ran through Tom. He could feel the bird's claws on his skin, and smell the strange hot, dry smell of his feathers. He sat still, hardly daring to move.

Sunny reached his shoulder and sat there for a moment. Daringly, Tom turned his head. The parrot gave a startled cheep and began to scramble down Tom's shirt sleeve.

'Sorry, Sunny,' whispered Tom. 'I didn't mean to scare you.'

Sunny had reached the end of his sleeve. He grabbed a beakful of material and let his body drop, so that he was swinging down, dangling by his beak.

'Idiot,' said Afra fondly. She put out her hand and Sunny climbed onto it.

Tom watched her. He was filled with a powerful envy, an almost physical longing. He wanted to own a parrot, to have one, to be its friend and carer, to teach it to do funny things and play with it for hours on end. He wanted it desperately.

'I wish he was mine,' was all he managed to say.

'Wish he was mine, too,' Afra said regretfully. 'I've only got him for a week.'

With a burst of energy, Sunny launched himself off Afra's finger and flew up to the perch she'd fixed for him, suspended from the roof of the cage. He turned his head away from them, as if he was waiting for them to go away.

'I guess he's tired,' said Afra. 'They're like that. They need a break. And it's nearly bedtime for him. Hey, let's go see if Sarah's made any cookies.'

Tom followed her reluctantly out of the cage. He looked up one last time, hoping that Sunny would give him, at the very least, a farewell bob of the head.

'Goodnight, Sunny,' he said softly.

With deep delight, he heard a gruff voice reply from the perch, 'G'night, ev'body. See ya tomorrow.'

He followed Afra up towards the house.

'You'll have him for how long?' he said. 'A week?'

'Yeah. Come and see him whenever you like.'

He grinned at her.

'Try stopping me.'

The shadows had been lengthening for some time now, and the glowing light of the late African afternoon was rapidly fading into the early African twilight. Tom sat down on the dusty steps of the veranda. Something small with a scaly tail darted out of sight beneath him.

Only a lizard, he thought placidly, not bothering to move. He'd have jumped up with fright a year ago, when he'd first come to Africa. He'd been scared of everything then, of snakes and spiders and shadows under trees. He remembered his old self incredulously. He hadn't even liked Africa! He'd thought of nothing but going back to England!

A flame of intense happiness, coming out of nowhere, shot through his heart, making him glow with joy. He felt good. He felt wonderful, in fact.

He looked round with a deep sense of satisfaction. He loved being here, in the Toveys' garden, with his two best mates and all their amazing animals.

He glanced up. The heat of the day was over now, and a cool breeze was fluttering the frayed and faded striped awning that covered the veranda. A flock of lovebirds was settling into the great mango tree at the bottom of the garden, their emerald bodies flashing among the dark leaves like brilliant tropical fish darting in and out of seaweed. A tail hung down from the roof of the veranda, where Kiksy, Afra's bushbaby, slept in his nest.

Joseph came round the corner of the house and sat down beside him.

'You liked the parrot, then?' he said.

'Liked him! He's amazing! I'm going to come and see him every day.'

Afra came out onto the veranda with a plateful of cookies. 'Guess what, Joseph,' she said. 'Sarah says your Uncle Titus was here today.'

Joseph looked up eagerly while Afra dropped cookies in his and Tom's outstretched hands.

'She told me he's going down to the coast next month,' Afra went on, 'to do a turtle survey. He says we can all come too, that is, if your mom and dad don't mind, Tom.'

Tom sat up.

'Turtles! Wow! They'd better not mind. I won't let them.'

Sounds from inside the house came faintly out through the veranda door, the clatter of saucepans and the rattle of utensils in a drawer. Sarah, who was Prof Tovey's housekeeper, was getting supper ready.

'I'd better go home,' said Tom, suddenly uneasy that he'd been out for too long. 'I'll come over after supper, if Mum'll let me.'

'We can do our homework together,' said Afra, who was in the same year at school as Tom. 'It's science tonight.'

'OK, see you.' Tom cranked himself up off the steps.

'Yeah, see you,' said the others.

Tom turned out of the Toveys' front gate and in through his own. It was always a strange sensation, moving from Afra's house to his. The wild garden and untidy, fascinating bungalow, full of books and strange old objects, was as different from his own neat, ordered house as a shaggy old dog was from a trim little cat. No weeds grew in the Wilkinsons' garden, and inside the house dust was ruthlessly excluded. Nature, in his mother's eyes, existed to be controlled.

Bella, Tom's four-year-old sister, was squatting beside the front door, her floppy yellow sunhat making her look like a large plucked flower.

'Mummy wants you. Mummy's looking for

you,' she said, turning reproachful blue eyes on him.

Tom ignored her, but a little of his glowing happiness faded.

He pushed open the front door and went straight through the little hall into the sitting room. Debbie had just finished feeding baby Jimmy. She had laid him against her shoulder and was rubbing his back to bring up the wind. Jimmy was sunk in a milky stupor, his head lolling sideways. Tom relaxed a bit. Mum looked too busy to worry about him.

'Hello love,' she said. 'Where have you been?'

'Homework. Next door,' Tom said succinctly. 'I haven't finished though. I'm going back after supper.'

'Hmm.' Debbie seemed about to say more, but Jimmy suddenly erupted in a loud burp, and she smiled with satisfaction. 'Dad'll be home in a minute. He's got some amazing news for you.'

'For me? What news?'

Debbie smiled.

'You'll see. I promised I wouldn't say.' She turned her head slightly at the sound of a car door slamming outside. 'Here he is now.'

Simon Wilkinson, Tom's dad, came in through the front door, dropping his jacket in a heap on the floor.

'Wow, it was hot in the car,' he said.

'Dad, Mum says you've got some news,' said Tom.

He felt a stirring of something inside him, and realized it was more like dread than excitement.

Simon advanced into the room, rubbing his hands.

'News! You bet. It'll blow your mind, Tom. I always told you Murchisons was a terrific company, didn't I? Well, they've come through with the goods this time. It looks as if that promotion I was hoping for is really going to happen. It means more travel for me, and maybe a six-month stint in South Africa for all of us. But listen! This is the best bit. They've offered to pay your school fees, Tom, and all your travel expenses, at a really top-notch school in England! Think of it! What an opportunity! It was plain old state primary and comprehensive for Debs and me, but you'll be getting the very best. You know how much you wanted to go back to England, Tom, to see your friend Scott and all your old mates again? Well, now you can. You'll be on the plane at half-term, in three weeks from now!'

# 2

# UNWELCOME NEWS

Tom stared at his father. He couldn't believe his ears.

'To England? You're going to send me back to England? On my own?'

His voice was squeaky with horror.

Simon was loosening his tie and undoing the top button of his shirt, but he was watching his son a little anxiously.

'Come on, Tom,' he said, with a slightly forced breeziness. 'You've been dying to get back to England. You moaned non-stop when we first came out here. You were ticking off the days till you could go home and see your friends.'

Tom's skin was prickling as the hairs on his arms and scalp stood on end.

'But that was at first! Ages ago! Dad, you're kidding. I'm not going anywhere. I'm staying here. I like it here. I *love* it here!'

'Listen, darling,' began Debbie. 'I know it seems a wrench for you, but . . .'

Tom ignored her.

'I'm going to be in the football team after

half-term, and Uncle Titus is going to take me and Joseph and Afra to—'

A disapproving frown settled on Debbie's face. 'That precious pair? Again? Oh no, Tom. Every time you go away with them something awful happens. You get charged by an elephant, or attacked by lions, or—'

'Mum, that's so unfair!' The panic welling up in Tom was clouding his brain. He couldn't think straight.

They don't mean it. They can't mean it! he kept saying inside his head. This is a nightmare. It's not happening. It's not true!

'Look, Tom,' said Simon, and the patient reasonableness in his voice was somehow more alarming, more definite, than the worst outburst of anger would have been. 'I know it's a surprise for you, and you'll take a bit of time to get used to it. You've done very well here. You've got some friends, and you've settled better than any of us. But you've got to think of the long term. I'm on contract here. We won't stay in Kenya for ever. You've got to get back into the English system sometime, and this is such a brilliant opportunity. Free private school education! Anyone would jump at the chance.'

Tom's knees suddenly felt weak, and he sank down onto the nearest chair, startling Tiger, his cat, who had been curled up on it in a contented ball.

'What is this school, anyway? What's so great about a private school? I'm not going, wherever it is. I wouldn't even go back to my old school, and you can't make me! I won't, that's all. I just won't!'

He could feel tears thickening his throat and he stopped.

Simon sat down in the chair opposite and leaned towards him, resting his elbows on his knees.

'It's a great place,' he said. 'This is such a chance for you, Tom. It isn't as if your mum and me haven't thought it all out. The school's called Uplands Grove. It's got fabulous facilities. A huge sports ground, and loads of activities, and you only have to share a bedroom with one other boy.'

'It's a *boarding* school?'

Tom was gripping the arms of his chair so hard that his knuckles were white.

'Only weekly boarding.' Simon's voice was hearty now. 'You sleep over from Sunday to Thursday night, and you go out on Friday.'

'Out? Where? What do you mean, out?'

'That's the beauty of it,' said Debbie, in a voice bright with jollity. 'Auntie Jean's offered to have you for the weekends. You've always liked Auntie Jean. Remember all those times she took you out when you were little, to that theme park, and to the panto at Christmas, and everything?'

Tom looked at her, unable to say a word. Then he turned to his father again. This time, he didn't bother to hide his tears.

'Dad,' he said, 'I'm not going. I'm just not. If you try to make me, I'm going to run away.'

He jumped up, and ran towards the door. He heard Simon's chair scrape on the floor as he stood up, and Debbie's voice say, 'Leave him, love. It's been a shock. Let him get used to the idea. He'll come round to it.'

Tom paused outside long enough to hear Simon say impatiently, 'Get used to it? I thought he'd be over the moon.' Then he ran upstairs, dashed into his bedroom and slammed the door as loudly as he could behind him.

In the days that followed, nightmare succeeded nightmare for Tom. Every night he went to bed with a pain gnawing at his insides. Every morning he woke up with a sinking sense of dread.

At first, he'd refused point-blank to talk about it, even with Afra and Joseph. Not even being with Sunny could comfort him. He'd gone next door every day after school, walking straight into Stumpy's cage where Sunny greeted him with enthusiastic squawks, climbing up his shirt front to his shoulder as he had done that first day, and gently tugging at his hair, as if he was preening the feathers of a fellow bird.

'I'm not going,' Tom would say to Afra, tightening his lips. 'No one can make me.'

'You will,' she'd answer. 'You'll have to, in the end.'

Joseph had said hardly anything, but by the way he'd refused to meet Tom's eye, Tom could see how upset he was.

For the first few days after Simon's bombshell, school had seemed almost the same, but bit by bit Tom had begun to feel as if he was becoming a non-person, a has-been. As if he'd died and become a ghost.

'Hands up who's going on next month's field trip to Nakuru,' one of the teachers would say. 'No, not you, Tom. You'll have left by then.'

'We went to Amboseli last weekend,' someone in his class would boast. 'It's brilliant there. You'd love it, Tom. Oh, sorry. I forgot. You won't be able to go now, will you?'

He'd tried everything at home. He'd had spectacular rows with Simon and Debbie, and then he'd tried days of stormy silence. Nothing had worked. It was a settled thing. He was going to school in England, and that was that.

It'll be like dying, thought Tom, one early morning, when, unable to sleep, he'd come downstairs to the empty sitting room.

He scooped Tiger up and nursed her in his arms. Outside, the sounds of an African dawn were breaking over the garden, the chirpings and

20

hootings and trillings of a hundred birds, and the whooping cries of the troop of monkeys who lived in the strip of forest beyond the garden fence.

Bella's favourite toy, a pink fluffy rabbit, was lying on the floor. Tom kicked at it savagely. One of the worst things was that Bella and Jimmy would still be here, still at home with Mum and Dad, breathing in the sweet warm air of Africa.

'And they don't even *appreciate* it,' muttered Tom.

He heard steps on the stairs. His dad was up and on his way to the kitchen.

'Can't I even stay till the end of term?' Tom called out to him despairingly. 'Why does it have to be so sudden?'

Simon appeared in the doorway, yawning and scratching his head, so that his hair stood up in spikes over his ears.

'You're up early,' he said. 'Can't you sleep?'

'No,' said Tom shortly. 'Didn't you hear me, Dad? Why can't it wait just till the end of term?'

Simon sighed.

'I told you, Tom,' he said patiently. 'It's all linked up with my promotion. If Murchisons get the South Africa contract, we'll be off in a month's time to Johannesburg. I don't see how we could take you with us, what with getting you into a school down there and everything.'

He turned and went on towards the kitchen. Tom followed him. Tiger jumped out of his arms and trotted ahead of Simon into the kitchen. She took up her usual position by the fridge door and began mewing loudly.

'Look.' Simon put an arm round Tom's hunched shoulders. 'I know you're unhappy about all this. Mum and I do understand. We really do. And we're not looking forward to losing you either. But you've just got to trust us on this one. It's a fantastic chance for you. It's for your own good.'

'I could stay here without you,' said Tom desperately. 'I could live with Afra. Prof wouldn't mind. He wouldn't even notice. And the school here's a really, really good one, Dad. I'd work harder, I promise. I'd do all my homework and you'd never have to nag me. I mean, maybe you didn't know, but Pierre's brother got a scholarship to Oxford from one of the schools here, and Yen Sung's sister won the gold medal in an international poetry competition. The schools in Nairobi are great! They're fantastic! Honestly, Dad, I bet you didn't realize that.'

Simon didn't answer. He was bending down to pour milk into Tiger's saucer.

'And Auntie Jean,' Tom went on desperately. 'Maybe she was just being polite. She won't want me hanging around all the time. I mean, what if she and Uncle Ted want to go away for the weekend, and they won't be able to because of me? It's not fair on them, Dad.'

Simon straightened up.

'Ah, yes, well. Jean. I was meaning to mention that to you, old son. The thing is, there's been a slight change of plan.'

'A change? You mean, you've decided not to—'

'I had an e-mail from Jean yesterday. She's had a stroke of luck, or at least, Ted has. He's got the job he's been after. A transfer to Scotland. It's what they've wanted for ages.'

'That's it then, isn't it?' A bud of hope was burgeoning in Tom's breast. 'I can't go if Auntie Jean can't have me at the weekend. I can stay here after all.'

''Fraid not,' said Simon, not meeting Tom's eyes. 'Jean's super-efficient, I'll say that for her. She's got these really nice neighbours, Paul and Cynthia Norris. They haven't got any kids of their own and they'd love to have you. Jean says they're great, really nice. Really keen on kids and everything.'

'What? *What*?' Tom stared at Simon, aghast. 'You're sending me off to live with total strangers? People you haven't even met? How do you know they're not serial killers or pervs or something? Dad, I just don't believe this! I just never thought you could do anything so – so mean, and cruel and *wicked*!'

# 3
# JAS


'Here we are,' said Debbie brightly, as she and Tom stood outside the door of a white bungalow, waiting for it to open. 'Wasn't it lucky I bumped into Bibi Singh at the post office? If I hadn't, we'd never have known that Jaswant was going on the same plane as you, and you'd have had to fly on your own.'

'Don't call her Jaswant. Everyone calls her Jas,' Tom said, scowling.

He hardly knew Jas Singh, who was a year ahead of him at school, and he didn't care if he had to travel with her or not. He'd only let Debbie drag him across Nairobi, using up half of one of the few precious days left to him, because he wanted to see Sunny, who'd been back with Mrs Singh for nearly a week now.

He looked round for any sign of the parrot, and thought he saw what looked like the corner of a cage, sticking out from the far side of the house. It was big, more like an aviary than a bird cage.

'I'm going to find Sunny,' he said abruptly, and dashed off before Debbie could stop him.

'Tom!' she called out sharply, but then the front door opened, and the sound of Mrs Singh's vociferous welcome faded as she drew Debbie inside the house.

The aviary was even bigger than Tom had thought. It stretched across from under a tall shady tree towards the side of the house. Tom looked through the grey wire mesh. He couldn't see anything. The aviary seemed empty.

'Sunny!' he called softly. 'Sunny, are you there?'

A piercing whistle, followed by a burst of incomprehensible parrot chatter came from overhead. Tom squinted up through the wire. Sunny had tucked himself away onto a high perch. He was turning his head from side to side, studying Tom, first through one eye then through the other. Then he lifted a claw and nibbled at it with the tip of his beak.

Tom craned his neck. It was difficult to see the parrot, right up there on his perch. He wanted to get closer, to feel Sunny's claws close round his finger, to stroke his soft feathers, as he had so often done in Afra's garden.

'Come on, Sunny,' he said. 'It's me, Tom.'

It mattered a lot, suddenly, that Sunny should come to him.

'Come on,' Tom pleaded. 'Hey, Sunny. What's the matter with you?'

'Nothing's the matter with him,' said a sarcastic

25

voice behind him. 'He only talks if he knows you, anyway.'

Tom turned round. Jas was standing behind him, frowning at him through her big glasses.

'I do know him,' Tom said indignantly. 'He came to me all the time when he was at the Toveys' house.'

Without answering, Jas walked round the side of the aviary towards a wood-framed mesh door. She undid the catch.

'Do you want to come inside?' she said.

'Thanks,' Tom said ungraciously, following her into the aviary. He didn't want to talk to Jas. He didn't know her well enough to like her or dislike her, but she seemed to be part of the plot that was closing in on him, tearing him away from Africa.

To his annoyance, Sunny launched himself at once off his perch and flew down to land on Jas's outstretched hand. He settled himself, preening his breast feathers, then stretched out one claw and with slow deliberation, began to walk up Jas's sleeve towards her shoulder.

'I'm going to get a parrot,' Tom said, surprising himself by voicing his secret wish out loud. 'I'm going to get one of my own.'

Her brows snapped together.

'Where? Where are you going to get one from?'

'Here, in Nairobi. You can buy them in town. Someone in my class told me.'

She clicked her tongue disapprovingly.

'You mustn't. You shouldn't.'

'Oh? Why not?'

She was really annoying him now.

'Don't you know where they come from?' she said. 'Don't you know it's awful to buy them?'

A red flush was rising in his cheeks.

'Who says?'

Sunny was trying to climb up her thick plait onto the top of her head. She winced as his sharp claws scratched her scalp.

'Sunny, stop that,' she said, pulling her head away.

'Who says it's awful?' Tom said again. 'You've got one.'

'We didn't *buy* him.' Jas's voice was scornful. 'My mum works for the KSPCA. They confiscated him when he was a chick from an illegal dealer. Sunny was really sick. He nearly died. They knew Mum would give him a good home, so they asked us to look after him.'

Tom said nothing.

'The KSPCA,' repeated Jas. 'The Kenya Society for the Prevention of Cruelty to Animals. Haven't you heard of them?'

Before Tom could answer, Sunny bent his head and dipped his beak down towards the pocket of Jas's blouse, spreading out his tail as he did so to display his lovely crimson tail feathers.

'Hey, Sunny, you're tickling my cheek!' said

Jas, moving her head sideways as the parrot's tail feathers brushed her face.

Tom watched enviously. The parrot's beak was inside Jas's pocket now, but he was overreaching himself. He lost his grip on Jas's shoulder, and grabbed at the edge of her pocket. He hung there for a moment, flapping his wings and scrabbling with his claws to get a hold on the material of her blouse. Then he scrambled back onto her shoulder.

'OK, Sunny, you win,' said Jas, and she reached down into her pocket and came up with a handful of dried melon seeds. 'I was saving these. I was going to eat them later.'

She showed the seeds to Sunny, then closed her hand over them again.

'You have to ask for them, Sunny. Go on. Ask.'

Sunny had stalked with ungainly strides down Jas's arm and was now perched on her wrist. He was bending his head, trying to prise the seeds out from between her clenched fingers.

'No,' said Jas. 'You have to ask. Ask, Sunny.'

'Gimme please,' said Sunny suddenly, and as Jas opened her palm, he screeched, snatched up a seed and snapped its hard shell expertly in his powerful beak.

Tom watched, entranced, his irritation with Jas momentarily forgotten.

'He's brilliant,' he said. 'I heard him talk at

Afra's. How did you get him to do it? I mean, say things that mean something?'

'Mum did it,' said Jas. 'She knows all about parrots. He does all sorts of amazing things for Mum.'

'How long have you had him?'

'We got him three years ago.' Jas was gently stroking the parrot's back as he tackled the second melon seed. 'He was young and sick. He'd been caught in the forest somewhere in Congo and smuggled into Kenya. He was half-dead.'

Tom frowned.

'You mean he's really a wild parrot? You shouldn't keep him! You ought to let him go!'

Jas shrugged.

'You can't, not once they've been taken away from their flock and the place they come from. He wouldn't last long on his own. There's no proper forest here and the hawks would get him.'

Sunny had launched himself off Jas's wrist. He had landed on the rim of his water bowl and was dipping his beak into it. Tom felt a swell of outrage.

'That's so horrible,' he said, looking at Jas, his dislike for her hardening in him again. 'You shouldn't catch wild things and send them away from their homes all on their own, and cage them up where they don't want to be, just so you can have a bit of fun with them.'

'Hey!' Jas frowned at him. Her glasses, too big

for her slim face, kept sliding down off her nose so that she had to constantly push them back into place again. 'You're the one who wants to buy a parrot, remember.'

'Not a wild one. Not one that's been caught,' Tom said indignantly. 'A tame one, that's been bred.'

Sunny strutted away from his water bowl towards the mess of melon seed shells by Jas's feet and picked one up in his beak. Bits of the shell shot out of his mouth as he bit his way through to the kernel.

Tom moved back towards the door of the cage, stumbled on a piece of wood and nearly fell, flailing his arms in an attempt to stay upright. Sunny squawked with fright and flew up to a high perch at the top of the cage.

'He won't come down now,' said Jas, annoyed. 'You scared him.'

'Sorry,' mumbled Tom.

Jas was opening the aviary door. Tom followed her out of it, and they walked in silence towards the house.

'If you just went off and bought one, how would you know whether it was a wild one, or one that's been bred?'

Jas was clearly unwilling to let the subject go.

'I'd ask the man who sells them,' said Tom uncomfortably. 'What do you take me for?'

He was beginning to feel as if he was in the

boxing ring and was being pushed back against the ropes.

Jas snorted.

'Dealers! They'd tell you anything. They don't care. They just want your money. It's really hard, breeding parrots. It's much easier trapping them in the wild. Do you know how they do it?'

'No,' Tom said unwillingly.

'The hunters go deep into the forest, and they put glue on sticks, and they put out food, and the parrots fly down and get stuck on the glue.'

Tom shuddered. 'That's really evil!'

'Yes.' His indignation seemed to have a molli-fying effect on Jas. 'And they pack them tightly into little boxes,' she went on, anger colouring her voice. 'They sell them here in Nairobi, and try and export them to Europe. They're not allowed by law to send more than a few, so they smuggle a whole lot more, illegally, and half of them die on the way, just so that people in England and places can have fun with a pet parrot in the house. They don't even have decent outdoor aviaries there, like we've got here, just little cages indoors. I know. I've seen them.'

They had stopped walking, and had turned towards each other. Tom felt irritation crackle fiercely through him.

'Not only England! I bet loads of other coun-tries get parrots that way too. And masses of people in Kenya have parrots in nasty little cages.

Anyway, the pet birds in England are bred there. My grandma had a cockateel, and she got him from a proper breeder.'

Jas pushed her glasses back up onto the bridge of her nose.

'Cockateels and budgies, maybe, but it's not so easy to breed African grey parrots. Bred ones cost thousands of pounds. It's cheaper just to go out and buy a wild one. How do people in England know, anyway, if they buy a bird in a pet shop, if it's been bred or caught in the wild? Most people wouldn't even bother to ask. They'd just buy the cheapest.'

The lofty superiority in her voice infuriated Tom, but he didn't know how to answer her. He frowned and turned his head away.

'Why are you going back to England, anyway?' asked Jas, changing the subject abruptly.

'They're sending me to school there.'

'Oh? Aren't the schools in Kenya good enough for you?'

Tom felt his face go burning red.

'Of course they are! Do you think I *want* to go? I'm going to hate it. And I'm going to hate leaving here, and I'm not going to enjoy travelling with you very much, either!'

As soon as the words were out, he regretted them, but unexpectedly, Jas began to laugh.

'You sound like my little cousin,' she said.

Tom ground his teeth, humiliated.

'No, really,' said Jas. She seemed to be looking at him for the first time, as if she'd only just seen him. 'Anyway, I know how you feel. Mum sent me to India on my own last year, to stay with my grandma for the whole summer. I didn't want to go at all. It was OK though, in the end. I liked it, actually.'

'Staying with your grandma's not exactly the same as going to a new school with a whole load of stuck-up kids you've never met before.' Tom was having trouble keeping tears out of his voice now.

'No. No, it isn't,' Jas said, more gently.

'What are you going to England for, anyway?' Tom said, to fill what threatened to become an awkward silence.

'My older sister lives in London,' said Jas. 'Well, it's Hounslow really. She's had a baby. She's asked me to visit her. I might be going there to study later. I'm going to be a lawyer.'

The calm certainty in her voice impressed Tom, in spite of himself.

'I'm only going for a couple of days, just for half-term. I'll be back at home here by the end of next week,' Jas went on.

'Lucky you,' said Tom sourly.

They had almost reached the front door. It opened, and Debbie came out, with Bibi Singh behind her.

'There you are, you two!' Debbie said brightly.

'Made friends, have you? That's lovely. Thanks for the tea, Bibi. We'll see you again on Friday, at the airport, when we send these two off on their big adventure!'

# 4

# SWEATFACE

Tom sat in the back of the car between Afra and Joseph, his shoulders hunched in misery. Simon was driving, but the front seat was empty. Jimmy had had a temperature that morning, and Debbie had had to stay at home with him.

Tom had nearly cried when he'd said goodbye to her. He'd wanted to cling to her, to scream and shout like Bella did, but pride and anger had made him stand rigid and still while she hugged and kissed him.

'You'll be all right, darling, I know you will,' she'd said, but he could hear the anxiety in her voice under a false veneer of confidence. It had sent an answering pang of dread through him.

He hadn't wanted to look back when Simon had driven out through the gate, but at the last minute he'd turned his head and seen her wiping her eyes.

Good, he'd thought, longing and anger battling inside him. I hope you cry all day.

He felt as if he was standing beside a huge black hole, a well of darkness, and that he was about to be pushed over the edge, and that he would fall and fall forever into nothingness. He dragged his mind back to the present and looked out of the window at the brightly flowering oleander bushes by the side of the road.

'I always knew you'd just disappear one day,' Afra said suddenly, bitterness in her voice. 'I didn't think it would be so sudden, that's all.'

'It's not my fault, exactly,' said Tom miserably.

'And you haven't even given me your address at this school place.'

'Oh, you won't need that,' said Simon breezily. 'They're all on e-mail at Uplands Grove. Got the most up-to-date software and computers in every classroom. You'll be able to send messages whizzing backwards and forwards sixteen times a day.'

'Yes, and have everyone else read your private business too,' Tom said. 'No thanks.'

They'd arrived at the airport now. Simon pulled up outside the long curved departures hall, and the three children jumped out. Tom went round to open the boot, and Joseph helped him to yank out his heavy suitcase.

'I'll park the car,' Simon said. 'I won't be a moment. Wait here.'

'Look,' Afra said awkwardly to Tom. 'It's not long till the holidays. You can come back and stay with us then.'

Tom looked down at his feet.

'I know.'

'And we'll get your address from Simon and

write all the time, won't we, Joseph? You'll be snowed under with all our letters. You'll have to dig your way out. And we'll send e-mails too, sort of coded ones, that won't give anything away.'

'I want to hear about everything you do,' Joseph said. 'What the school is like, and the sports, and the teachers.'

There was a hint of envy in his voice. It steadied Tom.

Joseph wouldn't make a fuss if he was going instead of me, he thought. He'd think it was brilliant.

He summoned up a smile.

'Tell you what,' he said. 'If I want to say something secret I'll have a go at writing it in Swahili.'

'But you can't speak Swahili,' objected Afra.

'I can a bit. More than the teachers there will be able to, anyway.'

'Look,' said Joseph. 'There's Jas.'

Mrs Singh, her gauzy scarf floating out behind her, was advancing towards them, pushing a trolley on which was balanced an enormous suitcase. Jas, walking beside her, was reading a book, weaving expertly in and out of the crowd of people as if she had two pairs of eyes, one for her book, and the other for finding her way.

'There you are!' A relieved smile broke out on Bibi Singh's plump face. 'Look at these terrible queues! We'd better get a place in one of them before they fill the plane up and send it off without you. Where's your father, Tom?'

'Parking the car,' said Tom.

His suitcase was almost too heavy to lift. He pushed it along the floor in the wake of Mrs Singh and her trolley towards the nearest queue of passengers. The last thrust nudged the case a little too far, and it hit the legs of the man in front. He turned round and glared at Tom.

'Watch what you're doing, can't you?' he said irritably.

His face was red, and the thin straggling blond hair on his forehead was damp with sweat.

'Sorry,' said Tom.

The man turned away again, and Tom made a face to Afra behind his back. She giggled. The man half turned, as if he was about to say something else, but seemed to think better of it. He pushed his hands down into the pockets of his overtight trousers, and his gold bracelet flopped down over his wrist.

'Great! You've found each other.' Simon had appeared now. He put a bag into Tom's hands. 'Mum got these for you. She didn't want you to have them till you got to the airport. They're for the journey, mostly.'

Tom wanted to hand the bag back again.

I'm not a little kid, he wanted to say. You can't bribe me. But he couldn't resist looking into the bag. There were a few packets of sweets (his favourites), a puzzle book, a couple of fancy pens, a novel and a cardboard box. He pulled the box out.

'Wow! A camera!' said Afra, impressed. 'That's so cool, Tom. Take masses of pictures, so we'll know what this torture chamber of yours looks like.'

Tom saw that his father was looking at him expectantly. He turned the box over in his hands, not knowing what to do with it. He didn't even know what he felt. Simon took the box from him.

'Look, I'll show you how it works,' he said eagerly. 'It's dead easy. There's a film in there already.'

He opened the box and lifted the little camera out. He held it up to his eye.

'Come on, all of you. Get in closer, and I'll take a picture. Smile!'

'Smile, Jas,' said Mrs Singh, nudging Jas. 'Smile!'

Jas looked up from her book for a moment and pulled the corners of her mouth up obediently. Tom turned his head away, his features frozen in disapproval. There was no way, no *way*, he'd give Dad the satisfaction of seeing him smile.

'There you go, Tom.' Simon put the camera into Tom's limp hands. 'Built-in flash and tele-photo lens, self-loading, fully automatic – you can't go wrong. There's even a couple of extra films in there too.'

Tom said nothing. Simon fell silent. No one spoke. No one knew what to say.

The queue was moving slowly up towards the counter. Simon tried to pick up Jas's suitcase, but could hardly heave it off the floor.

'What have you got in here, Jas?' he said. 'An entire library of books?'

'Oh, you know,' Bibi Singh said, with a little laugh. 'It's just a few things for the baby. Once you start buying them, it's impossible to stop.'

Jas looked up.

'I kept telling you, Mum, you can get Johnson's Baby Powder in England, you know.'

'Yes, well.' Bibi looked embarrassed. 'It's for my grandson, after all.'

Tom looked along the queue. Another fifteen minutes, maybe, and that would be that. He and Jas would be going through the barrier, past passport control, into the no-man's land of the departure lounge where none of the others would be allowed to follow. He'd have jumped over the edge. He'd be falling down into the black hole.

He looked round wildly, almost tempted to make a break for it, to bolt out of the airport building and start running. He could see himself racing down the road back into Nairobi, the ground flying away beneath him. Then the fantasy came to a shuddering halt.

I don't even know the way home, he thought.

He became aware that two men, some kind of

airport officials, judging by their uniforms, were approaching, and his heart, sensitive to the slightest hint that there might be a last minute reprieve, lifted in a tiny sensation of hope.

They're coming to find me, he thought. They're going to tell Dad I can't go.

But the officials stopped beside the man in front.

'Mr Waller?' they said. 'Mr Terry Waller?'

The man in front slowly turned his head. He was chewing gum, and he didn't bother to stop.

'Yeah?' he said. 'What do you want?'

The taller official was carrying a sheaf of documents. He tapped the top one with his forefinger.

'You are transporting a consignment of endangered wild animals on this flight,' he said. 'Is that correct?'

The man nodded.

'Yeah. Pythons. What of it? You've got the paperwork and everything. The CITES* stamp's on it. What more do you want?'

He turned to face the two men, and stuck out his elbows aggressively. Tom could see that his forearm, protruding from the short sleeve of his luridly patterned bush shirt, was red with sunburn and powerfully muscled.

The official was looking down at the document doubtfully.

* Convention on International Trade in Endangered Species

41

'This stamp,' he said. 'Where did you get it?'

'In Congo,' said the man impatiently. 'From the wildlife people of the Congo. Counterstamped by customs. Look there. See that signature? The consignment's from Congo, on its way to London. I'm only in transit in Nairobi. It's all in order — date, stamps, signatures, everything.'

The two officials looked at each other, and began to speak rapidly in Swahili, too quickly for Tom to understand anything. At last they turned away.

'All right, Mr Waller. Enjoy your flight,' one of them said.

As they left, Tom caught the expression on the man's face, a mixture of triumph and relief as he wiped the sweat from his forehead.

'What was all that about?' he said quietly to Joseph, as Terry Waller moved forward to the check-in desk and loaded his case onto the scales. 'It can't mean that guy's taking a whole load of pythons onto the plane. What if they get out?'

'They won't,' said Afra, who was frowning, and looking thoughtfully at the man's back. 'They don't go in the cabin with the passengers. There's a special heated hold for animals. They'll go in there. But you know what, I think there's something funny about all this.'

'Yes, there is,' nodded Joseph. 'Those two men were from customs, and they were suspicious about that guy's documents. They said the stamp doesn't look right. They think maybe the export licence is forged.'

'Why didn't they arrest him then?' said Tom.

'They didn't agree. One of them thought it looked OK. The other one wasn't sure. Then the sure one, he said, "Look, it's nearly the end of my shift, and I don't want to stay here for hours and have all this kind of fussing around," and the other one agreed. So they decided to let him go.'

Afra's eyes widened.

'That's awful! What if old Sweatface here's a smuggler, and he's taking those pythons out illegally? You'd better watch him, Tom. I've got a feeling there's something weird about that guy.'

The man had finished checking in now. He lifted the sports bag he was taking as hand luggage, slung his camera case carefully onto his shoulder, and walked away from the queue. Bibi Singh and Simon, who had been chatting together, looked round to call for Jas and Tom.

'Come on you two,' Bibi called out cheerfully. 'Time to check in. What do you prefer? Window seats or aisle seats? Jas, put that book away. Tom, where's your passport? Hurry up. The young lady's waiting.'

# 5

# GOODBYE TO NAIROBI

Tom felt almost breathless as he went up the escalator into the departure lounge. Things had happened in an odd kind of rush at the end. He'd said goodbye to Dad and Joseph and Afra, and everyone had said meaningless things like, 'It won't be long,' and 'Make sure you write,' and then he was through the doors, past the passport control desk and beyond any chance of turning back.

In spite of himself, he couldn't suppress a little thrill of excitement once the others were out of sight. He'd never gone on a proper journey without Mum and Dad before. It was the most grown-up thing he'd ever done.

Maybe it won't be so bad, he told himself.

The neon-lit departure area was more like a long corridor than a lounge. It curved round in a long slow bend, and was lined with little sales kiosks and snack bars. Jas looked up at one of the TV monitors hanging from the ceiling, screwing up her nose to keep her glasses on.

'We've got a while till they call the flight. I'm going to read.'

She sat down on one of the plastic chairs that lined the corridor and buried herself again in her book.

Tom sat down beside her. He pulled the novel out of the bag his father had given him and looked at the title. It didn't look too bad. It looked quite interesting in fact. He opened it, and read the first paragraph, but the words didn't seem to make any sense. He shut the book again. There was no point in trying to read. He couldn't possibly concentrate.

He looked along the corridor. There was a gift shop a little way along, with wooden carved animals, and strings of beads, and red Maasai *shukas** displayed in the window.

Tourist stuff, thought Tom.

Some way further down, though, he could see a more interesting window, with a display of cameras and walkmans and electronic goods.

'I'm going to look round,' he said to Jas. 'Will you look after my stuff?'

She looked up quickly, nodded, and went back to her book.

Tom walked down the corridor. There were quite a few people around, sunburnt European girls carrying little holidaymakers' shoulder bags, African businessmen with their serious-looking briefcases, and American couples wearing

---

* The red blankets that Maasai warriors wear

45

wide-brimmed safari hats. Pairs of airport policemen in crisp blue shirts and smart peaked hats strolled down the corridor, their heads held high, staring impassively at the passers-by.

It's not really like being in Kenya at all, thought Tom, except for the policemen's uniforms. It's not like anywhere.

He stopped outside the window display of electronic gadgets. He could see a camera that was just like his new one. The price made him whistle. For a moment, he was pleased, then he thought, It was guilt, that's why they spent so much. They were trying to buy me off.

Someone came up behind him and Tom saw, in the glass window, the reflection of a brightly patterned bush shirt. He turned round. The man from the check-in queue, the man Afra had called Sweatface, was frowning down at a display of binoculars. Tom edged away from him, and nearly tripped over his shoelace. He bent down to tie it, then stood up again. He'd half thought he'd go into the little booth to look at the racks of camcorders and stereo equipment, but he couldn't be bothered after all. He drifted back to his seat and sat down again next to Jas.

She turned the last page of her book, read the final paragraph, sighed deeply, and shut it.

'That was amazing,' she said. 'Wonderful. I just couldn't put it down till I'd read the last word.'

She slipped the book into her bag. Tom half

wanted to ask her about it, but it had looked like a book for adults and he didn't want to seem ignorant.

Jas turned to look at him, as if noticing him for the first time.

'Are you going to be warm enough? It'll be cold when we get to England. It's cold on the plane sometimes too.'

He felt affronted.

'I know that. It's not exactly my first time there. I lived in England till last year.' He patted his little rucksack. 'I've got warm stuff in here.'

She looked at him more closely, a wrinkle of concern on her forehead.

'Are you still upset, then, about going back? It's home for you though, isn't it?'

'I told you before,' said Tom. 'I like it here. I don't want to go anywhere.'

'OK.' She shrugged. 'But at least you'll have your family there.'

'That's just it,' Tom burst out. 'I'm not even going to see my family. My auntie was meant to be having me for the weekends, but she's moved to Scotland, and I'm going to be staying with some horrible people called Norris. Auntie Jean's not even meeting me at the airport.'

Jas looked sympathetic.

'That's awful,' she said. 'I thought at least you'd be going to people you know.'

The kindness in her voice brought a lump to

47

Tom's throat. He swallowed, and blinked furiously. Jas seemed to understand, and looked away tactfully.

*Gulf Air announces the departure of Flight GF108 to Abu Dhabi*, a loudspeaker nearby suddenly intoned.

Tom was glad of the diversion. He twisted round to look up at the departure and arrival TV monitors suspended from the ceiling above his head, and began to read off the names of the different destinations.

'I don't even know where half these places are,' he said, anxious to stay off awkward subjects. 'Dar-es-Salaam, I know that. It's Tanzania. But where's Sana'a?'

'Yemen, I think,' said Jas, who was craning her neck to look at the monitors too. 'I don't know where Yaoundé is, though.'

'That's Cameroon,' said Tom. 'It's on the other side of Africa, in the corner where the bulgy bit goes off to the left. I know it because I've got a big map of Africa in my bedroom. I learned all the capitals.'

He felt a little spurt of triumph.

'I can't see our flight. Where's it gone?' said Jas, who was still looking up at the screens.

'Next screen along. Look, we're third from the top now. Kenya Airways flight KY102 to London Heathrow.'

He sat back in his chair. Sweatface was in sight

again. He was walking backwards and forwards more purposefully than the other, casual tourists. He stopped almost in front of Tom and Jas, glanced up at the monitors, then checked his watch. He looked up and down the corridor, as if he was waiting for someone. He checked his watch again, and marched on.

'What's he so fussed about?' said Tom.

'Afraid he's going to miss his plane or something, I expect,' Jas said. 'People get really tense sometimes. I've known much worse than you. You're quite peaceful, really.'

'Thanks,' said Tom, pleased and surprised.

There was a sudden burst of noise as a pair of doors opposite the seats where Jas and Tom were sitting swung open and a crowd of people began to stream through it. Unlike the waiting passengers, who were strolling aimlessly about, they walked purposefully, looking around for the signs that pointed to the passport control and exit.

'They've come off a plane. They must have just landed,' said Tom.

'It'll be the Yaoundé one,' said Jas.

Tom watched idly as the passengers went past, their shoes clacking on the hard vinyl floor, rustling carrier bags full of duty-free goods swinging from their hands. Most of them were Africans, but they didn't look like Kenyan people. Some wore long flowing robes and little caps. Others wore business clothes that were somehow more elegant, more foreign, than the clothes the Kenyans wore.

'They're speaking French,' he said to Jas, surprised.

'They do, in Cameroon,' she said. 'Everyone speaks French there.'

The loudspeaker overhead burst into life again. *Kenya Airways announces the departure of Flight KY102 to London Heathrow*, the disembodied voice said. *Would passengers please proceed to Gate number 10 for immediate embarkation.*

Tom and Jas bent down to pick up their bags. Jas's had flopped open, and her book had fallen out. She reached under her chair to pick it up, and Tom stood up, waiting for her.

He could see Sweatface again now. To his surprise, the man seemed to have joined the stream of people walking towards the exit. He was pushing through them, as though he was trying to chase after someone at the front of the queue. Then, as Tom watched, he came up alongside an African in a blue safari suit. The man half turned and seemed to say something, then Sweatface fell into step beside him.

'Got your boarding card?' said Jas, standing up at last.

'Yeah,' said Tom, feeling in his pocket. Then a tingle of horror swept through him. The little strip of cardboard wasn't in his breast pocket, where he was sure he'd put it. He thrust his hands into his trouser pockets. It wasn't there. He searched feverishly through his little rucksack, and rifled through the bag Simon had given him.

'Don't tell me you've lost it!' Jas said resignedly.

'I haven't! I can't have! I had it just now!' said Tom.

He was beginning to panic. His heart was pounding and his hands were shaking. He had no idea what to do.

Jas was frowning, thinking things through.

'You went off for a bit while I was finishing my book,' she said. 'Perhaps you dropped it then.'

Tom's memory stirred. He had a fleeting impression of himself standing by the plate glass window of the electronic goods kiosk, looking at the cameras. He'd moved away when Terry Waller had appeared, then he'd bent down to tie up his shoelace. Perhaps something had fallen out of his pocket then. Come to think of it, he half remembered seeing something rectangular lying on the ground when he'd stood up again.

'Wait,' he said. 'I'll be right back.'

He took off and raced back towards the display window again, darting between startled passengers, hardly noticing their exclamations of disapproval. He arrived back at the plate glass window and stared down at the floor. Nothing was there.

His knees felt weak, and his stomach was fluttering. Then a wonderful thought came to him.

If I've lost my boarding card, I can't go on the plane. I can't go to England. They'll have to let me stay here!

He was standing, confused, not knowing what to think or what to do, when a young man came out of the booth.

'You are looking for something, I think,' the young man said. 'You have lost something?'

Tom turned to him.

'My boarding card.'

'What is your flight?' the young man said. 'Where is your destination?'

'Kenya Airways to London Heathrow,' said Tom. He knew already what the outcome would be. His heart was quietening down. The dizziness was ebbing away out of his head.

'Then you are so lucky!' the young man said, with a pleased smile. 'I have found your card for you. I kept it for you.'

He handed it to Tom with a flourish.

Tom took it. The moment of panic, then of hope and euphoria was over. He was back to harsh reality again.

'Thanks,' he said, turning away.

'Have a very delightful flight!' the young man called after him.

The crowd of passengers off the plane from Yaoundé was slowing to a trickle now. Along the half-empty corridor, Tom could see Sweatface again. He was standing by the wall, in conversation with the African man in the blue safari suit. They seemed to be arguing.

As Tom watched, the African put down the red carrier bag he was holding and reached into his pocket. Then both of them stopped and looked round. The pilot and the cabin crew, the last to disembark from the Yaoundé flight, were approaching along the corridor. They looked smart and official as they hurried along in their trim uniforms, pulling behind them their little wheeled suitcases. The pilot, his sleeves heavy with gold braid, walked in the middle of them, exuding an air of calm authority.

Beyond them, Tom could see Jas signalling to him. He trotted back to her.

'Have you got it?' she said.

'Yes.'

The anxious crease disappeared from her forehead.

'Don't do that to me again,' she said. 'I got really scared.'

They moved off towards the departure gate and, looking over his shoulder, Tom saw that the pilot and his crew had passed Sweatface and his companion and that the two of them were engaged once more in what seemed to be a furious row.

# 6

# MYSTERIOUS SOUNDS

There seemed to be a big crush of people queuing up to get on the plane, but when Jas and Tom had boarded, and had found their seats, they could see that it was only half full. A family with a couple of little kids was sitting near the front. One of them must have been Bella's age, about three or four years old. Tom looked at her almost longingly. He'd never, ever, have believed he could miss Bella, that he'd have liked to be sitting with her cuddled up against him while he read her a story, but that's suddenly how he felt. He *was* missing her. He was missing everyone and everything.

Jas was stowing her bag neatly in the overhead locker. She took Tom's from him and put it up too. It was obvious she'd been on long flights many times before.

'You can sit by the window if you like,' she said.

'Thanks.'

She stood back to let him get into his seat before she sat down. Tom was about to slide into the window seat when he saw Sweatface approach down the gangway. The man stopped a couple of rows ahead, and put his sports bag, his camera and his carrier bag carefully down on an empty seat. Tom's eyebrows rose in surprise. This carrier bag was red, like the one the man off the Yaoundé flight had been carrying. Tom was sure, though, that Sweatface had been carrying a white bag when he'd been queuing at the check-in desk.

He nudged Jas.

'There's that man,' he said. 'I saw him again when I went to look for my boarding card. He was having a row with some guy off the Yaoundé flight.'

'So what?' said Jas, uninterested. 'Aren't you going to sit down?'

'No, but look,' insisted Tom. 'He had a white bag when he was checking in. He's got a red one now, like the other guy had.'

Jas thought for a moment.

'That doesn't mean anything. He probably did some duty-free shopping or something. Look, are you going to sit down?'

Tom took a last glance at the man, who was sitting down himself now. He was peering into the red carrier bag as if checking that something inside it was all right.

Tom slid into the window seat and fastened his seat belt. He still had in his hand the bag his dad had given him and now he delved inside it.

'Want a sweet?' he asked Jas.

'Thanks.'

They unwrapped their sweets and sat in silence.

The huge, powerful engines were roaring to life as the great Boeing 747 began to taxi to the end of the runway. Tom, distracted by the business of boarding the plane and finding his seat, had been in a neutral state for the last half hour or so, but now that the yellow grass and blue horizon of Africa were beginning to race past the window in a final blur of speed, his sense of loss and fury came flooding back.

It's so mean of them. It's so unfair, he thought. It's just all wrong. I won't stay there. I won't!

He felt an almost physical pain, as if he was a plant that had been torn up by its roots.

The plane was airborne now. It was wheeling round in a great arc, tilting to one side, as it flew over the vast expanse of Nairobi National Park. Tom's nose was pressed to the window as he gazed down longingly, trying to imprint everything onto his memory.

The rains had been over for some while now, and the land below was brown. Animal tracks criss-crossed the huge bare plain, converging at a series of waterholes. There were buffaloes down there, Tom knew, and gazelle, and rhinos, giraffes, zebras, ostriches – lions and leopards even, the whole miraculous menagerie of Africa's great beasts, living and dying, fighting, playing and mating, leading their normal lives right alongside a great modern city.

He thought about the leopard he'd seen once, that had come right into his own back garden. What had happened to him? Had he found a new territory? Had the other leopards let him carve out a place for himself, or had they bullied him, and driven him on to look for somewhere new?

The park was disappearing rapidly now under the plane's wing, and nondescript brown land was taking its place. As the plane rose higher, Tom could make out less and less. Soon the land below would be only a dun-coloured blur.

He shivered. Jas had been right. The air conditioning was on full, and he was feeling cold.

He looked up. The seat belt sign had been switched off.

'Sorry,' he said to Jas. 'I'll have to get out. I need my sweater.'

She moved her legs aside and he scrambled past her. He reached up to the overhead locker, but it was too high for him, so he hopped up onto the empty seat in front.

'Are you OK? Do you need any help?'

A friendly young flight attendant had appeared from nowhere.

'I can't reach my bag,' mumbled Tom, embarrassed.

He jumped off the seat and waited further

down the aisle while the young man felt about in the locker for him.

'Is this the one?' he said, pulling out Tom's rucksack.

Tom nodded. He took it and rested it on the aisle seat of the central block while he opened it. Sweatface was in the window seat behind him, the red carrier bag on the empty place by his side.

Tom took out his sweater, did up the straps of the rucksack and handed it back to the flight attendant, but as he did so a strange noise caught his ear. It was a faint scrabbling sound, the sound of a shifting, scratching movement.

Tom looked behind him. There's something in that red bag, he thought, and it's alive.

He looked down at it, puzzled, then Sweatface's hand shot out and he pulled the bag closer towards him. At the same time he looked up and stared at Tom. The man's eyes were a cold, ice blue. There was no expression in them.

Tom turned away and put his sweater on. As he was pulling it down over his chest, the flight attendant said, 'Are you and the young lady travelling on your own? Unaccompanied?'

Tom nodded.

The flight attendant smiled.

'Would you like to visit the flight deck later and be shown round it by the pilot?'

Tom had an odd feeling that the attendant had noticed how unhappy he was, and that he was trying to make him feel better. He was afraid of being humoured, like a child, and for a moment he wanted to say no, in a dignified way, but the smile on the young man's face was so full of pure friendliness that his suspicion vanished.

'OK,' he said. 'Thanks.'

'I will come for you later, when we have settled more into the flight,' the attendant said, and he went off down the aisle.

I'm going to miss Swahili accents more than anything, Tom thought gloomily. No one in England's going to talk softly, and kind of up and down, the way Africans do.

He squeezed past Jas and sat down in his seat again.

Jas had pulled another book out of her bag and had started to read again. Tom wanted to tell her about the noise he'd heard, coming from Sweat-face's red bag, but after one look at her face he thought better of it. Jas was concentrating fiercely. He wouldn't get much out of her for the rest of the journey.

He sat and gazed vacantly ahead. A meal came. He ate a bit of it, not fancying anything much, and the remains were taken away. He tilted his chair back and sat still, slumped in a stupor of unhappiness, his mind revolving in a useless repetitive round of resentment and dread.

At last, when he thought the flight attendant

must have forgotten him, the young man came back.

'The captain can see you now,' he said.

'You go,' said Jas. 'I've been up on a flight deck before. I want to go on with my book.'

Tom followed the flight attendant to the front of the plane, then up a narrow stairway. He couldn't help enjoying a thrill of specialness. Several people looked up at him, clearly wondering why he was so privileged. He squared his shoulders a little.

Businessmen were occupying the wider seats on the upper deck. They were slumped in sleep, or reading bundles of papers, or sipping what looked like expensive drinks.

The flight attendant opened a small door at the front of the upper deck and ushered Tom through it. Tom nearly gasped. Rows and rows of dials and levers and instruments covered the whole ceiling and every square centimetre of wall in the cramped little area. The windows were tiny, and almost too high to see out of. A big man sat in one of the two seats. He was talking into the microphone attached to his headset.

'Khartoum, Khartoum, this is Kenya 102,' he was saying. 'Sierra Mike Lima 11.45. Flight level 350. Estimating November Whiskey Victor at 12.09.'

He flicked a switch and turned to look at Tom.

His face broke open in a grin as he took in Tom's expression of respectful awe.

'I'm Captain Njoroge,' he said. 'Who are you?'

'Tom Wilkinson,' said Tom shyly. 'How do you know what all these levers and stuff are?'

Captain Njoroge shrugged.

'I'm a pilot. It's my job.'

Tom looked at him. He was a big man, with the same air of quiet authority that the Cameroonian pilot had had as he'd walked down the corridor surrounded by his crew. A thought had been growing almost unnoticed in Tom's head. Now it suddenly burst out, surprising him.

'What would you do if there was something funny going on in your plane?' he said. 'Like a person smuggling a wild animal, or something like that?'

Captain Njoroge's eyebrows shot up.

'You are smuggling a wild animal?'

Tom shook his head and blushed.

'No, not me. But there's a man back there. He's got a box, and I thought I heard something in it.'

The captain smiled.

'You have been reading adventure stories, young man. The aeroplane is moving. Things move about in boxes with the movement we are making through the air. Don't be afraid. There won't be any poisonous snakes or lions or angry buffaloes on my plane, will there, David?'

He looked over Tom's shoulder to the flight

61

attendant, and winked. The flight attendant smiled indulgently.

They're patronizing me, Tom thought indignantly.

Captain Njoroge turned back to Tom.

'Here's an interesting fact for you,' he said. 'You can impress all your friends with it. Do you know that we are using up one gallon of petrol every single second?'

'No, I didn't know,' said Tom stiffly.

He wanted to get off the flight deck, to go back to his seat. The thought that had been crystallizing in his mind had become a near certainty now. Sweatface had an animal in the box he was looking after so carefully. Tom was sure of it. And the man coming off the flight from Yaoundé had passed it to him.

They're smugglers, thought Tom. They're smuggling something alive.

He was filled with a sense of outrage and a powerful determination. Some frightened little creature was hidden in that box. It had been wrenched away from its home and the other members of its species. It was being sent away from the warmth of Africa to a cold captivity in Europe. He wasn't going to let it happen. He was going to see to it that the creature, whatever it was, was rescued from its cruel imprisonment and sent back to where it belonged.

# 7

# A PLAN OF CAMPAIGN

When Tom arrived back at his seat, he could see at once that something had happened to Jas. She was looking out for him, playing nervously with the end of her plait. Her book was shut, and was stuck into the pouch in front of her.

'You've been a long time,' she said. 'What were you doing? Trying to fly the plane?'

He ignored her. She was like all the others. She didn't care if Sweatface had some living creature banged up in a little box. She didn't want to know.

He squeezed past her and sat down in his seat.

'Listen,' said Jas. 'Maybe you were right. I looked while you were gone.'

He turned towards her.

'What?'

'That man's red bag,' she said. 'I looked in it.'

'Sweatface's bag you mean?'

'Yes. I wanted to go to the toilet, and when I went past his seat I saw he'd gone too. So I bent down and pretended to do up my shoelace, right beside the red bag. I heard a noise too.'

A surge of relief welled up in Tom. He wasn't alone after all.

'What do you think it is?' he said eagerly.

'I don't know, but I bet there's something alive in there. I took a peek inside the bag. There's a cardboard box in it with airholes. I'm sure I saw something move. Something grey. It could have been something furry, or with feathers maybe. Then I saw the guy was coming back, and I had to pretend I'd dropped something, and came back here.'

'I knew it!' Tom felt a mixture of triumph and disgust. 'Didn't I tell you? He must have taken it off that man from Cameroon.'

He waited for Jas to acknowledge that he'd been right all along, but all she said was, 'If that's true, then it'll be a bird for sure. A parrot, I guess. An African grey, even, like Sunny. They sell for the highest prices.' She shuddered, as if the cruelty of it had only just hit her. 'African greys are the smugglers' favourites. They usually go for them.'

'What are we going to do?' said Tom, after a pause.

'Tell someone, of course,' she said. 'One of the cabin crew.'

Tom snorted.

'I tried that. I even tried to tell the captain, and that steward guy was listening. They both thought I was some silly kid making up stories.'

Jas looked at him dispassionately, and he

thought resentfully, she thinks I'm a silly kid too, but her face was thoughtful rather than dismissive.

'They don't want a fuss, that's all,' she said. 'They'd feel silly going up to a passenger and saying, "Excuse me, sir, but we want to check out the birds you've got in your bag." '

She had mimicked the bland official airline voice perfectly, and Tom smiled. They sat in thought for a moment.

'We can't do anything,' said Jas.

She moved her hand, and Tom thought she was about to reach for her book again.

'But we've got to!' he said. His sense of urgency had made him speak too loudly, and he lowered his voice, aware that other people nearby might be listening. 'This guy's a criminal, probably. I thought you said you wanted to be a lawyer. Funny kind of lawyer you're going to be, if you don't even want to catch a smuggler.'

'Hey, wait a minute.' Jas looked offended. 'A lawyer's not a policewoman, thank you. Lawyers don't go around arresting people. That's not their job.'

'OK then,' said Tom, thinking rapidly. 'Supposing it was your Sunny he'd got in there? I mean, it's probably Sunny's little brother or sister or cousin or something. Just think of Sunny, stuck in a dark little box, terrified, all alone and—'

'All right, all right, you don't have to go on

65

and on about it,' said Jas crossly. 'Why don't you read or have a sweet or something, and shut up and let me think?'

She pulled her book out of the pouch again and opened it, but instead of reading she stared straight ahead, flicking the bushy end of her plait backwards and forwards between her fingers. Words piled up in Tom's head, pleading, persuading, coaxing words. He wanted a partner. He needed her support. He didn't think he'd have the courage to do anything without her. But her expression was so forbidding that the words remained unsaid. He sat back in his chair and looked out of the window, down onto the puffy white clouds below.

It was a long flight to London. Tom gave up worrying about anything after a while. He went into an odd kind of mental limbo. He watched the movie on the little screen suspended from the cabin ceiling, and drank the juice the flight attendant brought round. It seemed after a while as if they'd been on the plane for years and years, and that they'd stay on it forever.

He had quite a jolt when, hours later, the fluting, sing-song voice of one of the cabin staff came over the intercom.

'Ladies and gentlemen, we will shortly be landing at Heathrow Airport. Kindly fasten your seat belts, fold your tables away, put your seats into the upright position and make sure your baggage is stowed away safely under the seat in front of you.'

Tom, whose mind had been wandering through some hazy landscape bathed in a golden southern light, felt an uncomfortable judder in his stomach. If he was going to do anything about Sweatface it was now or never. On top of that, he'd be meeting the Norrises in a few minutes. He'd know what he was in for.

The plane landed smoothly. Rain was lashing against the little window by Tom's seat, and the sky outside was lowering and grey.

London, thought Tom. This is it. I'm back.

He hadn't bargained for the rain. The reality of it, the normal Englishness of it, made everything to do with Sweatface and the bird in his box seem even more fantastic and impossible. Trussed-up birds, smuggled wild creatures, secret handovers in airports seemed somehow possible in Africa. They were quite incredible back here, in dull old London.

The plane stopped moving. Jas was already standing up and lifting down the bags.

She turned to Tom as he stood up, a crease between her brows.

'Look, I think I know what to do. You know after you've got your suitcase you go through the green channel if you haven't got anything to declare to customs, but you have to go through the red channel if you have? That's what we'll do.

We'll go through the red channel and tell one of the customs people to pick the guy up. Do a tip-off. Then it'll be up to them.'

'That's a really good idea,' said Tom, with grateful relief. The idea of simply reporting the problem to the very people whose business it was to catch smugglers hadn't even occurred to him. It was brilliant. Simple. Foolproof. Jas's calm, considered tone of voice was comforting too. It was bringing his tension down a notch.

She's in it with me then, he thought. She'll help.

'You've got a legal mind after all,' he said, relief lightening his voice. 'I'll hire you if ever I'm in trouble.'

Sweatface was taking his time, letting the other passengers gather their stuff up and get off the plane first.

He doesn't want people to jostle his bag, thought Tom, in case the poor little bird squawks or something.

He wanted to hang back too, but Jas prodded him in the back.

'Go on,' she hissed. 'We can't lose track of him. He's got to wait in the hall to pick up his baggage. We'll see him there.'

The walk from the plane to the passport control seemed endless. Tom kept wanting to look over his shoulder, to see if Sweatface was following, but he'd only done it once when Jas shot out at him, 'Don't look round! He'll get suspicious if he thinks we're watching him.'

There was a huge crowd in the baggage hall. Cases were already coming through on the long carousel from the Nairobi flight, and people were heaving them off and piling them onto trolleys. Tom looked round for Sweatface's lurid shirt, but he couldn't see it anywhere.

He's done a bunk already, he thought, his breath catching in his throat. We've lost him.

Then he caught sight of the familiar red face and lank blond hair. Sweatface had put a dingy-coloured bomber jacket on over his bush shirt, that was all. He was harder to spot in a crowd now.

Tom pointed him out to Jas. She pushed her glasses up her nose, narrowed her eyes to get a better view, and nodded.

'You watch him while I look out for our stuff,' she said. 'What's your case like? I can't remember.'

'Sort of black, with grey strap things round it,' said Tom, trying to visualize the suitcase, which his mum had packed, and which he'd never looked at properly. 'Oh yes, and it's got an orange sticker on the side.'

'Here's mine already,' said Jas. She plunged through the knot of people clustering by the carousel and lugged the heavy case off it. It was too big and awkward for her slim arms to control properly, and it banged against a trolley as she swung it clear of the conveyor belt. The trolley shot backwards and knocked into a smart young woman, who exclaimed in annoyance.

'Sorry,' Jas said, biting her lip with embarrassment.

Tom's attention had been taken away from Sweatface as he watched Jas's struggles, and when he looked up again, the man wasn't there. He'd been standing on the opposite side of the carousel only a few seconds ago, but now a knot of eager young people had taken his place, leaning over to grab their bulging backpacks off the conveyor belt.

Tom looked round wildly, but he was too short to see over the heads of the dense crowd of people in the baggage hall. He jumped up onto the nearest object that could give him a vantage point, the metal rim that edged the carousel's moving conveyor belt.

'Oi! Get off that!' a man in uniform called out. 'Don't you know it's dangerous?'

But Tom had leaped off already. He'd seen Sweatface, carrying his suitcase in one hand and the red carrier bag in the other, walking quickly down the baggage hall towards the exit.

'There he is!' Tom called out to Jas, who had at last managed to heave her case onto a trolley. 'And he's going through the green channel! Get my case and wait for me, Jas. I'm going after him!'

# 8

## HOT PURSUIT!

Tom darted through the crowd of people, every sense fully alert, dodging and diving between trolleys and pushchairs and piles of luggage. Sweatface was already halfway through the green channel when Tom dashed into the red one. A customs official was standing by a pillar, his arms folded, watching the crowd in the baggage hall.

'Hey, young man, where do you think you're going?' he called out. Tom skidded to a halt.

'Listen! Quick!' he panted. 'There's a man just gone through green. He's got a red carrier bag and there's a bird in it. I saw him get it off someone in Nairobi airport. The other guy was coming off a flight from Yaoundé.'

The customs man took this information in with gratifying speed.

'Right,' he said. 'You'd better show me. Come on. Let's go.'

Tom took off again, running out of the red channel, the customs officer at his heels. The electronic doors slid back, and he found himself facing a large crowd of people, who were standing behind a waist-high barricade, watching the new arrivals, waiting for the friends they had come to meet.

His own name leaped out at him. He had a fleeting impression of a middle-aged couple, with slightly anxious expressions on their faces, who were holding up a piece of cardboard with the words 'Tom Wilkinson' printed on it in thick black letters. He felt himself falter for a moment, but then he looked round for Sweatface again. He couldn't stop, even for a moment. Sweatface was walking fast. In a minute he'd be swallowed up by the crowd of people milling about in the arrivals hall.

Ahead of Tom and the customs officer a big family of home-coming holidaymakers, still in a carefree mood, were pushing three trolleys overflowing with suitcases, soft toys, plastic bags and sunhats. They suddenly saw the people who had come to meet them, and with loud shouts of greeting, slewed their trolleys sideways across the exit channel, right into Tom's and the customs officer's path. Tom felt a painful crack on his shin as he cannoned into one of the trolleys, tipping off a couple of cases. The holidaymakers apologized cheerfully, laughing as they helped the customs officer, who had almost fallen over, onto a steady keel again.

Tom hardly paused. His eyes were on Sweatface, who had reached the end of the barrier, and was walking off into the crowd. Tom craned his neck. The way ahead was blocked by more slow-moving people and their heavy trolleys of luggage. He could see at once what he had to do. He put a hand on the barricade and vaulted lightly over it. Then he was off again, flitting in and out through the crowd, in the direction Sweatface had gone.

He'd lost sight of him for a moment, then had to pull himself up sharply before he actually ran into him. Sweatface was standing at the bottom of an escalator, talking to a short, stout man in a brimmed brown felt hat and a green waxed jacket. He looked like a rich farmer type. As Tom watched, Sweatface handed the other man the red plastic bag and reached into the inner pocket of his bomber jacket. He pulled out the sheaf of papers and handed them over too.

'Here are your copies,' Tom heard him say. 'I'll meet you at the collection place when I've got the papers sorted.' They stepped onto the escalator and, still talking, were carried quickly up and away.

'Where did you run off to then?' said an irritated voice behind Tom. 'I thought I'd lost you.'

The customs man had arrived, panting with exertion.

'I was trying to keep up with him,' Tom said. 'Look, up there. Up the escalator. He's the guy in the grey bomber jacket.'

'Right,' the customs officer said, moving forward. 'Wait here, my lad.'

He ran up the escalator, taking the steps two at a time. Ignoring his instruction, Tom ran up after him.

Sweatface had stopped at the top. He was alone now. The man in the brown hat was walking nonchalantly away towards the lifts at the far end of the concourse, the red carrier bag in his hand. Sweatface had pulled a packet of cigarettes out of his pocket and was lighting one up. He looked up to blow out his first lungful of smoke, and saw the customs man approach him.

'Wait!' Tom lunged forward after the customs officer. 'Stop! It's not that man. He hasn't got the stuff any more. He gave it to—'

But the customs man didn't listen.

'Excuse me, sir,' he was saying to Sweatface. 'This is a no smoking area. Kindly put your cigarette out.'

'Oh, I'm sorry,' Sweatface said pleasantly, stubbing out his cigarette. 'I didn't realize.'

'Now then, sir,' the officer continued. 'I'm doing a spot check on hand baggage. May I see what you have in your bag please?'

Sweatface's eyes shifted once to the side, but he said, 'Certainly,' and raised his eyebrows in innocent surprise.

Tom could contain himself no longer.

'No, listen, he's handed it on,' he burst out,

tugging desperately at the customs man's sleeve. 'He passed his bag and his papers over to that man there, in the brown hat.'

The officer looked down at Tom, then back at Sweatface. Sweatface chuckled. The sound seemed so unnatural coming from him that it set Tom's teeth on edge.

'A bit too much imagination, I'm afraid,' Sweatface said, shaking his head indulgently. 'This kid was sitting behind me on the plane. The movie was rather a good cop thing, you know, smuggling stuff past the police and all that. I'm afraid young Tintin here's got real life mixed up with the movies.'

The customs man hesitated.

'Who's this man you think you saw then?' he said to Tom.

'Over there!' Tom gesticulated frantically towards the lifts. 'Oh, he's gone!'

Sweatface burst out laughing.

'Oh dear,' he said. 'What a shame. Never mind. It was a nice try. Going to be a cop when you grow up, are you?'

Tom felt a red tide rush through his head. He was almost dancing with fury, but Sweatface had already turned back to the customs officer.

'Can you tell me where the nearest phones are?' he said, putting on a matey, man-to-man voice. 'I've got to call the missus. I'm back a day earlier than expected. Been on a business trip in Kenya, for my sins.'

'Yes, of course. The phones are over there, sir,' the customs man said, pointing back along the concourse. He turned back to Tom, a frown settling on his face. 'Now look, you little pest—'

But Tom had already hared off again towards the lifts. He was looking round desperately for the brown hat.

He must have gone up in the lift, he thought, and he pounded his finger on the call button.

He stood there for a moment, seething with impatience. The customs man wasn't following him, thank goodness. He was making his way back through the crowd towards the customs desk.

The Norrises! thought Tom. If I don't get back there soon, they'll start going crazy.

Suddenly, his eyes focused on a distant sleek dark head with a familiar plait dangling from it. Jas had emerged from the baggage hall. She was holding onto a trolley laden with two huge suitcases, and was in earnest conversation with the middle-aged couple who had been holding up the card with Tom's name on it. Even from this distance, Tom could see that Jas's stance was defiant, and that the couple were looking stunned.

'She's found them then,' Tom thought, and a little relief momentarily lightened his anxiety.

He turned back to the lift. The doors remained

obstinately shut. His glimpse of Jas and the Norrises had started to sap his will-power, and he hesitated for a moment. He and Jas might have been wrong after all. Maybe there was something quite innocent in Sweatface's bag, a stuffed bird, or a toy for a kid or something. And even if there was a live bird in there, what could he do to help it? It must be valuable, or Sweatface wouldn't have gone to the risk of smuggling it into London, and if so, whoever got it in the end would have paid so much for it they'd be sure to look after it properly. It was a valuable piece of property. They wouldn't want it to die.

And then into Tom's mind flashed a picture of Sunny, bobbing his beautiful grey head, and taking off from his perch and flying in an easy swoop down to the rim of his water bowl. No one in England would keep a parrot in an aviary as big as Sunny's. It would be impossible indoors, and much too cold outside. No, the bird would end up in a tiny little cage, with a little rod to perch on, unable ever again to spread its wings and soar, condemned for ever to be cramped up and alone, an alien, a prisoner in solitary confinement.

I'm not, I'm just not going to let it happen, thought Tom.

The lift doors opened at last. There was only one button, fortunately. He pressed it and the doors swished shut.

He felt a brief moment of futile hopelessness while the lift went up. He'd been in airport car parks before. They were huge and anonymous and confusing. He'd never be able to find the man in the brown hat. He didn't even know which floor he'd be on, let alone in which section.

But he was in luck. He saw the brown hat almost as soon as the lift doors opened. The man was standing in the queue for the ticket machine, waiting to pay his car park fee before he went to find his car. He held the red bag in his hand.

Tom's heart lurched. He was still onto him, still in with a chance of tracking him, wherever he was going.

He felt suddenly conspicuous. A boy of his age, on his own, would stick out in a place like this. It would be awful if the man noticed him.

The lift doors behind him opened again and a family came out. There were a couple of kids younger than him. Tom moved quietly closer to them. Anyone casually looking round would assume he belonged to the family. They were perfect protective colouring.

The man in the brown hat reached the ticket machine at last. He fumbled in his pocket, pulled out some coins and retrieved his exit ticket from the machine. Then, without a backward glance, he began to walk quickly through the rows of parked cars.

Tom slid away from the family and followed

him, ready to duck down out of sight if the man should turn round. He was acting automatically now, filled with one steady purpose, to keep the red carrier bag in sight as long as he possibly could, and to find out where the man was taking it.

It wasn't until his quarry stopped beside a big red saloon car and started to feel in his pockets for the keys, that Tom asked himself what on earth he should do next.

I'll get his car number, anyway, he thought. Then I suppose I'll have to go back.

The man took out the papers that Sweatface had given him and checked something on them.

The pythons! Of course! thought Tom. He's got to pick up the pythons! That means he'll be going somewhere inside the airport, to the cargo place round the back.

He knew about the cargo areas. When they'd first gone to Kenya, they'd had to send Tiger on ahead. She'd had to travel on her own, and he'd been really worried about her. Dad had brought him along to the cargo buildings on the airport perimeter so that he could see she was being properly looked after, and that she'd have a nice cage to travel in.

A terrifyingly daring plan was in his mind now. If he could only get to the freight place with Brown Hat, as he now called the man in his mind, he'd have a real chance of rescuing the bird. The pythons' papers would have to be properly checked there, and there'd be nobody that Brown Hat could hand the red bag on to.

Brown Hat had unlocked the door of his car. As luck would have it, another car was reversing into the bay in front. The driver seemed inexperienced. He came a little too fast, and braked sharply, almost slamming into the front of Brown Hat's car. With an exclamation of annoyance, Brown Hat marched round to the front of his car to check if it had been hit, and began arguing with the other driver.

Tom thought again, for one awful moment, of the Norrises waiting for him in the arrivals hall, and of Jas, trying to hold them at bay.

I'm in real trouble anyway, he thought. It can't get much worse.

Brown Hat and the young man were still shouting at each other. In a moment of blinding clarity, Tom knew that he had to seize his chance. Before his courage had time to ebb away, he opened the back door of the car and hopped inside. Then he crouched down behind the driver's seat and waited, his heart hammering painfully inside his chest.

# 9

# BROWN HAT

Brown Hat jumped into the car, started the engine and began to back out of his parking space. Tom, crouching on the floor behind the driver's seat, squeezed his eyes tight shut and clenched his fists. He couldn't believe what he'd done.

Ever since he could remember, his mum and dad had drummed the same thing into his head.

'Never go with strangers. Never get into a stranger's car. Always be careful who you talk to.'

And now, here, without a second thought, he'd jumped right into the car of a man who was probably a criminal, in league with international smugglers, going off somewhere into the blue. And no one, not Jas, or the Norrises, or anyone else in the world, had the faintest idea where he was or what he was doing.

Wild plans rushed through his mind. He'd jump up, stick his fingers into the back of Brown Hat's head and say, 'I've got a gun. Stop the car.' Then, when the car had stopped, he'd make a dash for it. Or he'd make some kind of rattling, bumping, mechanical noise, so that Brown Hat would think there was something wrong with the engine, and stop to get out and look. Then Tom would grab the keys out of the ignition and do a runner. He was sure he'd outrun Brown Hat. The man had looked quite flabby and unfit.

One by one, the desperate schemes faded out of Tom's head. He couldn't do anything. He could only wait and keep as still as possible, and try not to sneeze or cough. Then, when they got to wherever the man was going, he'd creep out of the car and find a police station or something, and hope that they'd help him track down the Norrises, who must be doing their nuts by now, in Terminal Three.

The car had speeded up once it was out of the car park. Tom didn't dare sit up to look out of the window, but by the sound of it they were out on a main road. It was still raining. He could hear the ping of the raindrops hitting the windscreen at speed, and the swish of the wipers. His heart sank even further. Why had he assumed they'd be going straight to the cargo area to pick up the pythons? They might be on a motorway by now. They might be going anywhere, to Wales, or Scotland even.

He was beginning to think that the tension would kill him, that he wouldn't be able to bear it any longer, when the car slowed down and pulled up. Brown Hat opened the door and got out.

This is it, thought Tom, curling into an even

smaller ball. He'll see me when he turns to lock the door.

But he heard Brown Hat's feet walk away from the car, and then there was a click as the locks engaged.

He's done it by remote, thought Tom, gasping with relief. He waited for a moment, then, with infinite caution, he raised his head. The car was in a small parking lot outside a two-storey brick building. The words 'Animal Reception Centre' were on a board above the door.

Tom whispered a triumphant, 'Yes!'

He'd been right. Brown Hat had come to pick the snakes up. He was still inside Heathrow, and here, at this place that dealt with animals, someone would believe the story Tom had to tell. Someone would rescue the bird.

He waited, watching, while Brown Hat pressed a buzzer, and a man opened the door from inside to let him in. His fingers slippery with nervous sweat, Tom pulled at the door handle. For a moment, he was afraid that it wouldn't unlock from the inside, but it swung open, and he almost fell out onto the ground.

He hadn't realized how cramped he'd been, crouching down behind the front seat, and his legs almost collapsed under him, but he gave himself a good shake and ran over to the door through which Brown Hat had disappeared.

He pressed the buzzer and waited. For what

seemed like an eternity nothing happened, but at last a tall young man, whose long soft brown hair was tied back in a ponytail, and who was wearing a T-shirt with a tiger printed on it, opened the door. He looked down at Tom, his eyebrows raised in surprise.

'Who are you?' he said.

'I'm Tom,' said Tom, 'but it doesn't matter. There's a man here, he came in just now. In a brown hat. He's a smuggler. He's got this box in his car. I saw him get it off this man in Nairobi—'

'Hey, slow down,' the young man said. 'What on earth are you on about? What man? What box? Start again.'

Tom looked up at him despairingly. No one else had listened to him. No one had wanted to believe him, not the pilot, or the flight attendant, or the customs man at Terminal Three, or even Jas, to begin with.

'It's a long story,' he said weakly. He could feel tears pricking inside his eyelids.

The young man suddenly seemed to realize that Tom was still standing out in the rain. He took his arm and pulled him inside. Tom looked around anxiously. Brown Hat wasn't here, in the small hall, but he could hear voices coming from behind a nearby door.

The young man sat down on a chair and patted the one beside him.

'From the beginning,' he said. 'Here's a tissue. And my name's Rob.'

Tom blew his nose and stuffed the wet tissue into his pocket. He'd have to talk fast and get his story right. At any moment, Brown Hat might come out of the office, and get into his car, and drive away with the bird still in the box.

'I've just arrived from Nairobi,' he said carefully, trying to put his thoughts in order.

'On your own?' Rob's eyebrows went up again.

'No, with Jas,' said Tom. 'She's a girl. She's come to England to see her sister.'

'Wait a minute,' said Rob. 'This Jas, she's a minor too? You don't have an adult with you? What did you come to England for?'

'It's OK,' Tom said impatiently. 'I'm supposed to be going to school here. Anyway, I've got to tell you, there was this man at Nairobi in the queue for checking in. His name was Terry something, Walker or Waller I think. And the customs men came up and asked about the papers he had because he was airfreighting some pythons. They were talking in Swahili, and my friend Joseph, he's African and he speaks Swahili, he said the men thought the papers were dodgy but they, the customs guys I mean, were at the end of their shift and they didn't want any hassle, so they decided not to bother. They just let it go.'

'Pythons, right,' said Rob, who was clearly trying to hang on to the gist of Tom's story. His brown eyes were warm and friendly. Encouraged, Tom went on.

'Anyway, while we were waiting to get on the plane, me and Jas, I mean, this flight from Yaoundé came through, and I saw Sweatface—'

'Sweatface?'

'That's what I called him, the man with the pythons, because he had a sweaty face.'

'Poor guy can't help having a sweaty face,' said Rob. 'You're cruel, you kids are. What would you call me? Bulgy nose? Floppy ears?'

He was grinning broadly.

He doesn't believe me, thought Tom, his confidence shrivelling again. He thinks I'm just a crazy kid.

Frustration welled up in him.

'Listen,' he said. 'You've got to listen! This guy, Walker or Waller or whatever, he swapped his bag with a man off the Yaoundé flight, and I heard something in it while I was on the plane, a kind of rustling noise, and Jas looked and she saw something grey like feathers through an airhole. He had a bird in there.'

The smile vanished from Rob's face. He was listening closely now.

'Ah,' he said. 'That's interesting. So what did you—'

'I'm telling you,' said Tom. 'I followed Sweat— the man, out of the baggage hall, and I saw him hand the bag to the man who came in here just now. The man in the brown hat. So I followed him, the man in the brown hat, I mean, to the car park, and when he wasn't looking I jumped into the back of his car and came here.'

Rob's jaw had dropped in astonishment.

'You did *what*?'

'I *told* you.' Tom could hear chairs scraping back behind the door. Brown Hat would be coming out any minute now. 'Look, you've got to believe me. You've *got* to! There's a red carrier bag in that car out there, and there's a box in it, and there's a bird in that box, and it's come all the way from Yaoundé, and it must be all trussed up, because it wasn't flapping around or squawking or anything even when the guy was swinging the bag around.'

The friendly, amused expression had disappeared from Rob's face. He looked quite stern suddenly.

'Right,' he said. 'Stay here, Tom. I'll be back.'

He disappeared into the room from which the sounds of conversation were coming. Tom, listening as hard as he could, heard only the murmur of voices at first, and then, as the door handle turned, an angry voice burst out, 'This is absurd! You have no powers to search my personal possessions. I'm here on a simple collection job. As soon as my colleague's got the papers endorsed, we're going to pick up the snakes.'

The door opened, and three men emerged from

the room. The first was Brown Hat, his stout face red with anger. After him came an official in a navy blue suit, and behind them both came Rob. He winked at Tom, then put a finger to his lips.

'You're mistaken, sir,' the man in the suit said, in the cool tones of officialdom. 'I am a customs officer and I have full powers of search. We have received information that you are in possession of contraband goods. Kindly accompany me to your car.'

'But this is outrageous!' blustered Brown Hat. 'I haven't even been abroad. I came up from Devizes this morning. I—'

'Your keys sir, please,' the customs man said, with icy politeness.

The three of them walked out into the rain. Tom ran to the door and watched as Brown Hat, still arguing, clicked the remote control. Before either of the others moved, he opened the door to the passenger seat and removed the red carrier bag.

'There,' Tom heard him say. 'Search the ruddy car. I'm going back inside, out of the rain.'

'First hand me your bag please,' the customs man said, holding out his hand.

'Why? It's got my tea in there!' expostulated Brown Hat. 'My sandwiches! Now, if you'll excuse me, I'll go and eat them in peace while you take my car to bits. And much good will it do you. You'll find nothing except for a few old sweet wrappers. Then I suppose you'll want to arrest me for littering my own car.'

The customs man said nothing. He simply stood there with his hands held out, waiting for Brown Hat to pass him the bag.

As Tom watched, everything seemed to happen at once. Brown Hat dropped the bag on the ground, and made a dash for the door of the driver's seat. The customs man leaped forward, and in an instant had him in an armlock. Then he twisted Brown Hat round till his head was bent down over the roof of the car, and extracted the keys from his hand. Rob, with a cry of outrage, had rushed forward to pick up the box, and was carrying it carefully back into the building.

The fight had gone out of Brown Hat. As Tom watched, he seemed to sag, and when the customs man took his arm and led him back towards the building, he came without a protest. A moment later, all four of them were standing in the office leading off the hallway.

Rob took out of the red bag a small cardboard box, no bigger than a large sandwich tin, and put it down on the table. Carefully, he lifted the lid. Tom leaned forward to see. Inside the box lay not one but three birds. Their beaks were bound with sticky tape. They had been pushed into surgical tubes of gauze to immobilize them, but one of them had scratched through his wrapping with his claw, which, even now, he was waving feebly in the air.

With infinite gentleness, Rob picked up one of the birds and peeled back the lower part of the gauze to show a flash of flame-coloured feathers among the duller grey ones.

'African grey parrots,' he said, 'and the first charge we'll get on you is cruelty.'

'I had no idea.' Brown Hat was putting on a fair show of horrified surprise. 'Honestly, a chap I know passed me the bag and asked me to look after it for him.'

'You said you had your tea in it,' said Tom, unable to stay silent any longer. He'd been keeping quiet and still with increasing difficulty. Triumph and disgust were swilling around inside him. 'Anyway, why did you try to run away just now?'

Brown Hat glared at him.

'What's that kid doing in here?'

Rob snorted and seemed about to say something, but the customs officer intervened.

'Mr George Lawson,' he said, and Tom heard Brown Hat's real name for the first time. 'I am arresting you on a charge of illegally smuggling a Category Two endangered species, and on a second count of cruelty. You do not have to say anything, but it may harm your defence if you do not mention when questioned something which

you later rely on in court. Anything you say may
be given in evidence.'

Rob turned to Tom.

'In other words,' he said, with jubilant smile,
'he's nicked. You're a star, Tom.'

# 10

# LIVING CONTRABAND

'Right,' the customs officer said, looking at Tom. 'Let's get to the bottom of this. I'm Jeff Stokes. What's your name, lad?'

'Tom,' said Tom. 'Tom Wilkinson.' He couldn't stop a huge grin spreading over his face. He'd been right all along, and he'd taken a massive risk, and it had paid off.

'And how did you get mixed up in all of this?' Mr Stokes wasn't smiling back. He was a small man, but everything, from the close-cropped hair on his round head to the polish on his soft black leather shoes, gave off an indefinable message of authority.

Tom's grin faded a little. He launched into his story again. Mr Stokes listened with growing incredulity, and George Lawson, who had taken off his brown hat to reveal a head of straggly thin grey hair, stared at him with increasing fury.

'You're telling me that you bolted out of the customs hall, leaving your baggage unclaimed, followed your suspect, witnessed the exchange, pursued this man here, climbed into his car without his knowledge and accompanied him to this place?'

'Yes,' said Tom cautiously. The story sounded unbelievable even to himself, and the way Mr Stokes said it, it was probably illegal too.

'I told you,' said Rob, who was leaning over the box and examining the parrots as closely as he could without touching them. He looked over at Tom with an expression of something like pride, as if Tom was his protegé and his exploits cast reflected glory on himself.

Mr Stokes shook his head, a smile of reluctant admiration twisting the corners of his mouth.

'Most impressive,' he said. 'How old are you? Twelve? Thirteen? Quite a hero. Glad you're not my son, though. You must give your mum and dad a right old runaround. Where are they? Who's supposed to be looking after you?'

Tom's grin had dropped altogether, and an anxious look had taken its place.

'My family's all in Nairobi,' he said. 'I told you. I was with this girl, Jas. Jaswant Singh. She's a bit older than me. These people I don't know called Norris were supposed to be meeting me. Actually, they did meet me, I think, because I saw a sign with my name on it, but I couldn't stop and talk to them because I was chasing Sweat— this other man, so – so I suppose they might be wondering where I am.'

'Might be wondering where you are?'

marvelled Mr Stokes, removing his smart blue jacket as if he was about to get down to work, and leaning his crisp white cuffs on the desk. 'I'll bet they're creating pandemonium by now. Which terminal were these poor souls waiting at?'

'Three,' said Tom unhappily.

Mr Stokes turned to the telephone and dialled a number.

'Is that you, Pete?' he said. 'Can you put a call out in Terminal Three? Got a lad here who's got himself over to animal reception on his own. Straight off his plane. His people are waiting for him. Name of Norris. Call me back, will you?'

George Lawson stood up casually.

'You got a toilet here?'

Mr Stokes nodded.

'We have. And no, you can't go. Not unaccompanied. You can wait till I've sorted this little lot. Oh, and just in case you get any funny ideas—' He fished into his pocket with his free hand and pulled out a pair of handcuffs. 'Cuff him, Rob.'

Lawson stared at Rob. He was pale now, and his eyes were moving to and fro as if he was trying desperately to think of a way out of the mess he was in, but he put his hands out obediently, and Rob slipped the handcuffs over his wrists and clicked them securely shut.

Then Rob turned his attention back to the parrots.

'I must get these on their feet again,' he said. 'It's going to take a while. I'd better get started.'

He moved towards the door, the box in his hands. Tom felt as if his only friend was deserting him. His face must have given his feelings away because Rob said, 'Is it OK if Tom comes with me, Jeff? It'll take a bit of time to get his people here. He might as well make himself useful.'

Mr Stokes, the receiver clamped to his ear, nodded, and Tom, relieved to be away from the threatening presence of Brown Hat, followed Rob out of the room.

Rob led him through into a vestibule, where white overalls and rubber boots were ranged against the wall.

'Quarantine regs,' he said. 'Get an overall on, and some boots, and look, over there, a mask to put over your face.'

Tom stared.

'A mask? Why?'

'Psitticosis. It's a lung disease wild birds have sometimes. People can catch it off them. It can kill them, too.'

Tom found the smallest overall and the smallest boots, but they were still too big on him. He felt like an idiot as he tied the mask on over his face.

'Here, hold these.'

Rob handed him the box of birds and quickly dressed himself, then he took the box back, and Tom followed him down a corridor.

He could tell at once that animals were kept here. There was a zoo kind of smell, and from the rooms that led off on each side came a jumble of rustlings, gruntings and bird calls. Through the window in one door, he caught a glimpse of a monkey, hunched in the corner of a cage. From another, came some ear-splitting squawks.

'Macaws,' Rob said. 'A whole suitcase of them. Intercepted them last week on the way into the country from South America. Half of them died, but the others are settling down nicely now.'

'What are you going to do with them?' asked Tom, peering fascinated through the glass at the aviary full of handsome black birds.

'Don't know yet. We'll have to find somewhere really good for them to go. They're special, these birds are.'

Tom smiled to himself.

I bet you think all the animals here are special, he thought. You're a real softie with animals, I can tell.

Rob, still holding the box of birds carefully in his hands, nodded towards a door leading off the corridor.

'The surgery,' he said. 'Open the door, will you?'

Tom held the door open and followed Rob inside. The surgery was a small room with shelves along one side. Bottles of medicines were arranged on them and in the middle was what looked like an operating table.

Rob put the box down carefully on the table.

'We'll have to go slowly,' he said. 'These birds are deeply traumatized. They'll be terrified of us, the room, the strange sounds, the lights – everything. Wait here with them, Tom. I'll have to get a cage to release them into.'

He hurried out of the room.

Tom approached the table cautiously. He hadn't had the chance to get a good look at the parrots yet. The three birds lay on their backs. One of them, the one that had poked its claw through its gauze wrapping, was turning its head, looking from side to side. The other two lay still, their eyes glazed and dull.

A noise behind him made Tom start, and he looked round. There was a big plastic tank in the corner of the room, and a kind of dry, scrabbling noise was coming from it. Tom went over and looked into it.

A crocodile, a metre and a half long, lay inside, its brown tail curved round its hindlegs, its forelegs splayed out as it tried to get a hold on the slippery plastic sides of the tank.

Rob came back into the room.

'You've met Mac, the croc, then,' he said. 'I'm keeping him in here under observation. He's better today. A lot livelier.'

'Where did he come from?' said Tom. He'd

never liked crocodiles. They were so sneaky, the way they hid in the water, and grabbed at anything that came near. He'd felt scared once or twice, in Africa, when he'd gone near a river bank, in case a huge pair of jaws might shoot out suddenly and catch him by the legs. But Rob clucked affectionately towards the big tank.

'I wish I knew where he'd come from,' he said. 'He was found in a telephone box in Hounslow. Someone must have had him as a baby. They're really cute when they've just hatched out, but they grow and grow. This lad'll get to be four or five metres long. I suppose his owners took a long look into the future one day and decided to dump him.'

'That's awful!' said Tom indignantly.

Rob was carefully cutting the gauze off the first parrot with a pair of sharp scissors.

'Amazing, isn't it? People do the weirdest, cruellest things with animals. They have no respect. They just don't *think*. I can't understand why human beings decide they have the right to own exotic creatures from other parts of the world, to deprive them of their natural habitat and their liberty, for their own selfish pleasure. It's indecent.'

He had released both of the parrot's wings now, and he was cradling the bird in his hand.

'It must have been scary for the person who found poor old Mac,' he went on, speaking softly so as not to alarm the parrot. 'Just think, you're going to phone your girlfriend, and you open the door of the telephone box, and there's this thumping great croc inside. Here, come and hold this little fellow for me, will you, while I get the tape off his beak?'

Tom took the little body from Rob's hands. The bird felt frighteningly light and fragile. He could feel the outline of its flesh under its soft feathers. He was afraid of hurting it, and at the same time filled with awe. He was holding a wild thing in his hands, a bird which, until a few days ago, had lived in the canopy of the great Central African forest, a creature of light and air and wind.

'Will he be all right?' he said. 'Will he get over all this?'

'Get over it?' Rob was working on the beak now, holding the bird's head with one hand and deftly stripping the sticky tape off it with the other. The parrot was straining to be free, trying to wrench his beak open. 'Of course he won't get over it. He's been kidnapped, imprisoned, condemned to captivity for the rest of his life. He'll never be free, or fly with a flock again. But he might live. I reckon we can save his life. He's a fighter, this one is.'

'I could take him back with me,' said Tom, inspired by the thought, 'and release him back into the wild.'

99

Rob shook his head.

'That's the awful thing,' he said. 'You can't send them back to the forest. For one thing, they might well be caught again. For another, this experience sometimes triggers latent diseases, and if they develop they can infect whole populations of birds. No, he'll have to stay, now he's here.'

He peeled off the last piece of tape and opened the door of the little cage, still holding the parrot's head to keep the wickedly sharp black beak from lunging for his hands. Together, he and Tom placed the bird on the perch in the cage and quickly withdrew their hands.

The parrot sat still for a moment, then he began ruffling out his feathers, looking at Rob and Tom first out of one eye, then out of the other.

'He's trying to threaten us,' said Rob. 'He's going, "Look at me. I am one scary big bird." '

The parrot dipped his head and began wiping his beak backwards and forwards on the perch.

'Cleaning himself up,' said Rob. 'He'll see the water in a moment. He must be desperately thirsty. Yes, look. There he goes. He'll be OK for a bit. Let's get going on the others.'

The second parrot was more listless than the first. He barely moved as Rob snipped the gauze off him and began working to free his beak.

'Badly dehydrated,' said Rob. 'We'll have a bit more trouble getting this little fellow back on his feet.'

Tom felt the difference as he held the bird in his hands. The life force that had flowed through the first parrot seemed strangely absent. The feathers were limp and the eyes dull. The bird croaked feebly as the tape was at last removed from its beak, and when they'd released it into the cage, it clung to the perch with both feet and sat, its wings drooping, its feathers fluffed up, as if it didn't care whether it lived or died.

'I'll have to get some water into him,' said Rob, as if to himself. 'Let's get the third one sorted first.'

They'd just finished working on the third parrot, and put him in the cage, when Mr Stokes put his head round the door. His cool, official manner had dropped away, and he looked almost excited.

'Guess what,' he said. 'The pythons have arrived, over from Terminal Three, and so has George's sweaty-faced friend. You were right, Tom. His name's Waller. Terry Waller. Our Mr Waller has been clearing his paperwork over at the airline office, and now he's come to help his little chum take possession of the snakes. He didn't realize he was walking into trouble. I've cautioned him and cuffed him, and he looks as sick as a parrot.'

Rob looked up at him reproachfully.

'Oh sorry,' Mr Stokes went on, unable to keep the broad smile off his face. 'Didn't mean to be tactless. I want you to go over that case of pythons with extreme thoroughness, Rob. Looks as if there might be an extra compartment underneath it. Oh, and we've sent a message out to contact your people over in Terminal Three, Tom, but I think we're going to need you to hang around here a bit longer. I'd like to hear your story all over again, every single detail of it.'

# 11

# A BOX OF SNAKES

Tom was sorry to leave the surgery, and to take off his boots and overall. He'd felt safe with Rob, as if he too was an animal that had lost its way and been taken into Rob's care. He told himself sternly not to be silly, and followed Mr Stokes back into the office block.

Mr Stokes's questions seemed to go on for a long time, and he kept asking the same things over and over again. Could Tom describe the man at Nairobi airport who'd handed the bag over to Terry Waller? Was he sure that the plane had come from Yaoundé? Did he remember the flight number? Had Waller spoken to or had contact with anyone else?

At last he seemed satisfied. Outside, darkness was falling. It was getting late.

Tom sat back, exhausted.

'I expect you could do with a cup of tea or something,' said Mr Stokes.

Tom nodded. He was, now he came to think of it, extremely thirsty, and quite hungry, too.

Mr Stokes went out and came back a moment later with a mug of tea and a Mars Bar.

'I'm afraid I'll need you to identify Mr Waller,' he said, 'just to make certain we're investigating the right man. It's OK. We won't leave you alone with him. Finish your tea, and I'll take you back to the animal holding section. We're about to open his famous box of pythons, and he's been taken over there to witness it.'

'What about Mr Lawson?' said Tom. He didn't feel he could face two angry men at the same time.

'Don't worry about him. He's gone off already. The police sent a van over and they've taken him off to the nick in Hounslow. They've left two more men here, to keep an eye on Waller.'

There was quite a crowd of people in the corridor in the animal holding section of the building. Sweatface was the first person Tom saw. He was standing between a couple of policemen, and his face looked hotter than ever, his expression full of defiance and outrage. He didn't notice Tom.

Rob was bending down over a long flat wooden crate, prising the lid off it with a claw hammer.

'This is all totally crazy,' Sweatface was saying. 'I'm a perfectly legal importer of wildlife. You say you've found irregularities in my papers, but I can assure you, you're totally mistaken. And whatever you think about that bloke, Lawson, or whatever you said his name was, I keep telling you, I've never seen him before in my—'

His eyes fell on Tom, and his mouth snapped shut into a thin furious line.

'You've seen this man before?' Mr Stokes asked Tom.

'Yes.' Tom swallowed. The malevolence in Sweatface's eyes was horrible to see. 'I saw him swap bags with that man I told you about in Nairobi. I sat behind him on the plane, and then I saw him hand his bag over to the other man, Mr Lawson, at Terminal Three.'

Sweatface managed to laugh.

'This is the kid who pursued me out of the baggage hall,' he said contemptuously. 'The boy's crazy. Been watching too many films. Over-heated imagination.'

A loud splitting, tearing noise interrupted him as the wooden lid came off the crate. Tom involuntarily stepped back, afraid that a mass of snakes would come writhing out of it. He was relieved to see that the policemen, too, had moved surreptiously backwards, and were staring down at the open case with fascinated repugnance.

He needn't have worried. The case was divided into neat compartments, and in each one was nothing but a muslin bag.

'You see?' Sweatface said, licking his lips. 'Ten pythons. Packed in accordance with international regulations. They're exactly what it says in the papers.'

Rob didn't answer. He had picked up the first

bag with a pair of tongs. Deftly, he removed the clip that fastened it at the neck and carried it over to a large plastic tub. Then, holding the bag at the base, he turned it over and began to tip the contents into the tub.

A shower of shredded paper fell out, and after it emerged the first coil of a slim black snake.

'Careful, Rob!' said Mr Stokes urgently. 'That's no python!'

The snake seemed reluctant to leave its bag. It coiled back on itself, its head rising up perilously close to Rob's hand.

'Drop it, Rob! It's going for you!' cried Mr Stokes.

But Rob, with one lightning move, caught the snake just behind the head, holding it gently but firmly with the forefinger and thumb of his left hand while he released the rest of its muscular body from the bag with his right hand.

'A black mamba,' he said softly. 'One of the deadliest snakes in the world.'

He put the snake down in the tub and let its head go. The snake lay still for a moment, and then began to work its way round the tub, sliding up the sides as far as it could, then slipping back again, looking for a way out.

Tom's first feeling had been a kind of shuddering horror, an instinctive, primitive loathing. But as he watched the little animal, its head darting from side to side, its body sliding helplessly over the smooth plastic, he began to feel sorry for it. This creature too, like the parrots, had lived freely in its own place, had no doubt learned its own familiar territory. Though it was still young and small, it must have made itself a home in a hole in the ground, or in a hollow tree, perhaps. It must have moved and hunted and sought out its own kind as every living thing should have the right to do. And in spite of the fear its deathly load of poison would always inspire, it had a kind of beauty, too.

'And where is your dangerous animals licence?' Mr Stokes was asking Sweatface, his voice dry and expressionless.

Sweatface was staring down at the mamba with a pretence of open-mouthed astonishment.

'I had no idea,' he said, shaking his head wonderingly. 'My supplier's pulled a fast one on me. Pythons, he said they were. All of them.'

'Open the other bags later, Rob,' said Mr Stokes. 'Just remove them from the case. I want to have a good look at the bottom of it.'

Rob fetched a trolley from a nearby room and, one by one, put the muslin snake bags on it, handling them gingerly with the tongs. Then he tapped on the bottom of the empty case.

'Hollow,' he said, without looking up.

There was silence as he levered off the central thin plank of wood. Even the policemen craned forward, half-fearful, half-fascinated, to see what might be hidden in the dark cavity.

Tom held his breath. There could be more snakes in there, or other, faster things, with hairy legs, spiders perhaps, that might shoot out suddenly, and run up his leg and . . .

'Watch it, Rob.' Mr Stokes was clearly feeling nervous too, but Rob, peering into the false bottom of the case, exclaimed suddenly, and reached his hand in to pull something out of the hole.

He held the creature out to show the others. It was a little soft-shelled tortoise, no more than 10 centimetres long. Its head and legs were retracted into its shell and it lay as still as a flat pebble on Rob's hand.

Rob looked at Sweatface and his eyes were blazing.

'I hope you get ten years for this,' he said.

Tom could see that there was something odd about the tortoise. He leaned forward to look. A rod had been inserted through the rim of shell above the tortoise's head. It was fixed into the bottom part of the shell below the tortoise's lower jaw, so that the creature's nose bumped into it every time it tried to push its head out.

'But why?' said Tom.

'Because if tortoises can't put their heads out, they can't put their legs out either,' said Rob savagely. 'They have to keep still. They're immobilized. They won't give the game away.'

Tom looked up at Sweatface with disgust. A grey pallor was settling over the man's face. He put up a hand to wipe away the sweat that was still pouring off his forehead. As he did so, something caught Tom's attention. Sweatface's bomber jacket had fallen open, and Tom could see, quite clearly, that something was moving, something appeared to be wriggling, under his shirt.

'Look!' he said, pointing.

Sweatface had dropped his hand now and was quickly zipping up his bomber jacket.

'He's got something under his shirt,' said Tom. 'I saw it move!'

The policeman standing next to Sweatface took an automatic step away from him. Mr Stokes looked sharply at Tom as if wondering whether, after all, his imagination really had got the better of him at last, but Tom, not daring to look at Sweatface again, nodded vociferously.

'Honestly,' he said. 'I saw it.'

'Right,' Mr Stokes said crisply to Sweatface. 'Your jacket please sir.'

For an awful moment, Tom thought that Sweatface was going to leap right over the splintered case, with its cavity full of tortoises, shove to one side the trolley with its load of unidentified snakes, and go for him with his bare hands, but the policemen suddenly moved, and each of them grabbed Sweatface by the arms.

'Help him off with his jacket,' said Mr Stokes, sounding tired. 'Then we'll start on the rest of his baggage. We'll have to go through this guy's stuff with a toothcomb.'

Sweatface shook himself free, and, his face impassive again, took off his bomber jacket to reveal his bush shirt. Mr Stokes looked pained, as if the lurid pattern was hurting his eyes.

'Off,' he said. 'The shirt off too.'

Tom, wondering why he hadn't noticed it before, could see now that the shirt hung in a strange way, not straight down from the shoulders, like most shirts did. The bright pattern cleverly disguised the fact that it was covering something else, something lumpy and bumpy, something that was now definitely moving.

Reluctantly, Sweatface undid his buttons and took his shirt off. Tom gasped. Strapped round the man's chest was a heavy canvas kind of waistcoat. It was obviously several centimetres thick.

Mr Stokes stepped forwards and peeled back the top layer of the waistcoat, which was fastened to the rest with strips of velcro. Underneath it was a series of little pockets, and struggling out of two of them, cheeping raucously, were a couple of newly hatched chicks.

Even Rob couldn't help joining in the laughter that had spontaneously broken out.

'Birds' eggs,' said Mr Stokes, with deep satisfaction. 'Bit over ambitious, weren't you, Waller? Parrots, poisonous snakes, tortoises and birds' eggs, all on one trip? No doubt these chicks are some endangered species too. Pity you didn't remember that eggs have an uncomfortable habit of hatching.'

He lifted the waistcoat off the now unresisting Sweatface, who stood naked to the waist, a thinner, much weedier man than he had seemed to be five minutes earlier.

Mr Stokes laid the waistcoat carefully down on a bench. Tom could see that it was cleverly constructed. A series of little pockets, reinforced with strong plastic linings, were hidden under the jacket's outer covering. Nearly every pocket contained a bird's egg.

'I'll get these straight into the incubator,' said Rob.

He picked up the jacket, then wrinkled his nose. Even from a distance Tom could see that it was dark and damp with perspiration.

That's why he's so sweaty! thought Tom with satisfaction, pleased that another piece of the jigsaw had fallen into place. Sweatface must have been boiling hot, wearing that thing all the time.

A door behind him opened and he looked round. Another policeman had appeared.

'Anyone called Tom Wilkinson here?' he said. 'I've got a Mr and Mrs Norris to see him. I couldn't hold them at Terminal Three any longer. They insisted on coming right over here to fetch him themselves.'

# 12

# THE NORRISES

Tom sat in the back of the Norrises' car, staring unseeingly out of the window into the dimly lit streets of a south London suburb. It seemed like hours since they'd all climbed silently into this old-fashioned Ford.

He'd realized, the minute he'd seen Mr and Mrs Norris standing in a state of twittering anxiety in the vestibule of the Animal Reception Centre, that his stay with them would be awful. Miserable. Totally depressing.

They hadn't been angry with him. They hadn't blown up, or asked him what the hell he thought he'd been up to, or told him he was a damned nuisance, or ticked him off for worrying them sick.

Mr Norris had said, 'Well, I don't know what to make of it all, do you, Cynthia?' and he'd shot a nervous glance at his wife. She'd said, 'Least said soonest mended. We'll pretend this never happened, Tom. We don't want to start off on the wrong foot, do we?'

He'd tried to tell them. He'd tried to explain that he hadn't meant to be difficult, or to upset them, but it was perfectly obvious that such things as assignations at Nairobi airport, smugglers, parrots, black mambas and waistcoats with secret compartments full of hatching chicks would be so far outside the Norrises' realm of experience that they'd never, in a million years, understand any of it. When he'd started to explain, they simply hadn't believed him. Or else, Tom had thought sulkily, they'd presumed he was actually involved in criminal activities himself.

Not even Mr Stokes's 'Well done, Tom. You did a great job,' or the policemen's cheery waves impressed them. Mrs Norris only said, 'I hope you won't get mixed up with the police again, Tom,' in a repressive voice, that seemed to indicate that she feared and expected the worst of him.

The car pulled up in a quiet street. Little Edwardian houses in continuous terraces lined it on each side. The Norrises' house, unlike the neighbours', had a high privet hedge separating the tiny front garden from the street.

Tom trod up the cracked cement path after Mrs Norris, and waited, feeling miserably out of place, as Mr Norris fumbled in his pocket for his front door key. He looked up at the dingy façade of the house, feeling as if he was looking at his prison. He could see the word 'Roseneath' in faded painted letters on the window above the door.

It was the smell of the house that struck him

first. There was nothing really bad or unwholesome about it, but it made him wrinkle his nose in disgust. It was an old smell, a kind of mustiness, a smell of damp carpets and boiled vegetables and worn clothes. It told Tom at first sniff that no one young, no one lively and noisy and energetic, had lived in the house for years and years.

'Take his case up to his room for him, Paul,' said Mrs Norris, putting on a bright voice. 'My, whatever have you got in that thing, Tom?' She watched as her husband began to struggle up the stairs and called up to him more sharply, 'Mind you don't do your back in again.'

She went down to the end of the corridor.

'Come on into the kitchen, Tom,' she said. 'I know they always give you far too much to eat on planes, but I expect you'd like a little supper before you go to bed. Look at the time! Half-past eight already! Way past your bedtime, I expect.'

Tom followed her into the kitchen. It was scrupulously clean and tidy but everything, from the formica-topped table to the white enamel electric cooker, looked dowdy and staid, as if it had been there for forty years at least.

'Sit down, dear,' said Mrs Norris. 'Oh no, what am I thinking of? You haven't washed your hands! Upstairs on the half landing. Come down as soon as you're ready.'

Mr Norris was already in the kitchen as Tom came down the stairs again.

'I don't know what boys like these days, Cynthia,' Tom heard him say, 'but I'm sure he'll like it. I used to love cold tongue.'

'Now then, Tom, sit down,' Mrs Norris said, looking at Tom nervously.

There was only one place laid at the table.

'Aren't you going to have any?' Tom said, looking up to see both Norrises watching him as if he was an exhibit at the zoo.

'No. We eat early as a rule,' Mrs Norris said. 'What do you want to drink? Water? Milk? A cup of tea?'

Tom was looking down at the plate in front of him. On it was set a couple of slices of some purplish cold meat, a few limp lettuce leaves and half a hard-boiled egg. A roll of white bread was on the smaller plate beside it. He looked up again. An awful feeling of desolation was sweeping over him.

'Tea, yes please,' he managed to say.

'And there's a bit of a treat for afters,' said Mrs Norris. 'Stewed rhubarb and tinned rice pudding. Eat up now, Tom. Goodness me, it'll be time for the nine o'clock news in a minute.'

Tom picked up his knife and fork and put a lettuce leaf into his mouth. He'd thought he was hungry. In the car, he'd imagined a warm cosy kitchen, and a tasty piece of pizza, or a hamburger and some chips, but this cold supper was turning his stomach. The half hard-boiled egg seemed to look up at him like a moist dead eye, and the meat looked weird and slimy. He ate the bread, finished the lettuce, and pushed his plate away.

'Oh dear, I hope you're not going to be picky with your food,' said Mrs Norris. 'Normally we don't get pudding if we haven't eaten our first course, but seeing as it's your first night, we'll make an exception.'

She put a plate of cold rice pudding in a puddle of pink rhubarb down in front of him.

In the next room, Tom could hear Mr Norris fiddling with the answerphone. There were a couple of beeps, and then a familiar voice said, 'Paul? Cynthia? Jean here. Just calling to see if Tom's arrived safely. I'll call later.'

Tom felt a stab of longing. Auntie Jean was family. Last time he'd heard her voice, they'd all been together, just before he'd gone off to Kenya for the first time with Mum and Dad and Bella. Auntie Jean had been wishing Mum luck, and laughing with Dad, and blowing kisses at Bella. A wave of longing for his family, and his home, and for Afra and Joseph and Stumpy and Kiksy and the whole continent of Africa washed over him.

If I was at Auntie Jean's place, it wouldn't be so bad, he thought.

Auntie Jean and Uncle Ted were great. They cooked mounds of brilliant food, and Uncle Ted put his feet on the table, and burped, if he felt like it, and Auntie Jean was always saying to Mum, 'Debbie, ease up on Tom. You're too hard on him.'

The beeps started again and Auntie Jean's voice said, 'Cynthia? Still not back? Jean again. I'll call around nine.'

Tom ate a mouthful of cold rice pudding. It wasn't as bad as he'd expected and he was so hungry he found he could eat it after all. He finished the plateful, put his spoon down and looked up.

Mrs Norris whipped the bowl out from under his nose at once and put it down on the spotless draining board.

'Paul!' she called out. 'Tom's finished his supper. Show him the lounge and dining room, and then he can get off to bed.'

Mr Norris appeared at the door. He'd taken his jacket off and was dressed in a sagging cardigan and bedroom slippers.

'Come on, Tom,' he said.

Tom followed him back up the corridor and in through the first door on the right. A highly polished table stood in the middle of the room with six chairs set round it. Against one wall was a matching sideboard. The room was cold and cheerless.

'We don't use the dining room much,' said Mr Norris. 'Auntie Cynthia thought you could do your homework in here.' He looked down at

Tom, a puzzled crease between his brows. 'You'll have plenty of homework, I expect. It's one of those academic schools, isn't it?' He smiled, trying to look encouraging. 'Don't worry. I'm sure you're a very bright lad. You'll show 'em all, won't you?'

Tom didn't answer. Mr Norris went out of the dining room, closing the door carefully after Tom, and opened the next door along.

'Here's the lounge,' he said.

The two armchairs on either side of the fireplace, and the sofa that made up the three piece suite were a little too large for the small room, but it had a certain cosiness to it. There was a big TV in one corner and some brightly coloured pictures on the walls.

'You can watch TV in here with us,' said Mr Norris, shaking Tom's shoulder playfully. 'We'll fight over which programme to watch, eh?'

Tom smiled, embarrassed, and wriggled out of Mr Norris's reach.

'Who's that?' he said, pointing to a large framed photograph of a little girl, that stood on the mantelpiece.

Mr Norris cleared his throat.

'That's – that was our little Bethany,' he said. 'Our little girl. She passed on many years ago. Don't mention her to Auntie, Tom. It upsets her to talk about it.'

The telephone on the little table by the window

rang again, making Tom jump. Mr Norris answered it.

'Oh Jean, yes!' he said. Tom could hear his aunt's hearty voice crackling at the other end of the wire. 'No, the plane wasn't late. Best not to enquire too closely what kept us so long. We've agreed with Tom to let bygones be bygones. No, he's here. Yes, I'll ask him.' He turned to Tom. 'It's your Auntie Jean, Tom. Do you want to speak to her?'

Tom almost bounded across the cramped little room and had to restrain himself from snatching the receiver out of Mr Norris's hand.

'Tom!' Auntie Jean's voice sounded wonderfully real and solid and familiar. 'What on earth happened? Are you all right?'

Tom looked round, and saw with relief that Mr Norris was leaving the room.

'Oh, Auntie Jean,' he said, and then found he couldn't go on. His throat was too thick with tears.

'Tom?' Auntie Jean was saying. 'Are you there? Are you all right? Tom!'

'Yes,' he managed to say. 'I'm all right. I didn't do anything wrong at the airport, Auntie Jean, honestly. There were these men. They were smuggling parrots.'

'What? What did you say? Speak up. This line's awful.'

Tom gave up the attempt.

'Nothing,' he said. 'I didn't say anything.'

There was a pause.

'When do you start at your new school?' said Auntie Jean, her voice sounding more subdued.

'Monday,' said Tom, choking back tears again.

'You've got a few days, then, to settle in.'

'Yes.'

'I'll phone your mum tomorrow and tell her you've arrived safely. They'll all be asleep by now, with the time difference and everything.'

'Yes.'

'Tom, you're OK aren't you?' She sounded anxious. 'You're getting on with Paul and Cynthia all right? I know they're a bit quiet, but they're lovely people. Hearts of gold.'

There was a short silence.

'It's all right,' whispered Tom. 'Goodnight, Auntie Jean.'

## 13

## JAS TO THE RESCUE

Tom lay in bed the next morning and looked round the little room. He shut his eyes again at once, trying to conjure up his room in Nairobi, with the big elephant poster at the bottom of his bed, and dark green leaves tapping against the window, and the heady scent of the frangipani tree by the kitchen door which wafted into the whole house in the morning.

There was nothing nice about this horrible little room, with its pale green walls and musty smell of mothballs. It had obviously been a kind of junk room and had only recently been cleared out.

For me, I suppose, he thought sourly.

There were rawl plugs still in the wall where shelves had been taken down, the curtains didn't quite reach the window sill and a pile of cardboard cartons was piled by the door.

From the bathroom on the other side of the wall by his bed he could hear the toilet being flushed. He turned over onto his face and pulled the pillow over his head. If he really, really concentrated, perhaps this nightmare would stop. Perhaps he'd find himself back once more in his room at home, staring into the huge mango tree outside his window where monkeys sometimes played and he'd often seen chameleons.

There was a tap on the door.

'Tom?' said Mrs Norris. 'Are you awake? Breakfast's ready. It's half-past eight already. You've had your lie-in.'

The Norrises were already sitting down at the table when he went into the kitchen.

'Top of the morning to you, Tom,' said Mr Norris. 'No need to ask how you slept. A gift of youth, sleep is. Enjoy it while you can.'

He had milk stains on his moustache. Tom averted his eyes. He sat down at the empty place. He had no idea what to say.

'We have All-Bran as a rule,' said Mrs Norris, 'but I bought you some Rice Krispies. Children like them, don't they?'

'Snap, crackle and pop, eh, Tom?' said Mr Norris, with a horribly jovial wink.

'Oh yes. Thanks,' said Tom.

He'd never felt much about Rice Krispies before, either for or against, but he knew he'd never eat them voluntarily again.

'Now,' said Mrs Norris, pouring out a cup of tea. 'What are we going to do with you today, Tom? The school want you to go in tomorrow, to meet your new teachers and get your uniform at the school shop and see round the place, but you've got a free day today.'

'Oh you don't need to worry, Cynth,' said Mr Norris. 'I'm going to take Tom up the canal. Do a bit of fishing.'

'Oh please,' burst out Tom desperately, 'please Mrs Norris, can I phone my friend Scott? He doesn't live very far away. He was my best friend before I went to Africa.'

Mrs Norris's face cleared.

'Oh yes. Scott. Your mum wrote about him. She said you'd want to get in touch with him straight away. Finish your breakfast, Tom, then you can go into the lounge and call him.'

'And if he's at home I can go round to his place, can't I?' Tom felt like a man in a dark forest who could see a beam of light in the distance through the trees.

'We'll see,' said Mrs Norris. 'Scott's mother might have other plans.'

'She works,' said Tom. 'Scott's on his own mostly, in the holidays.'

Mr and Mrs Norris exchanged disapproving looks.

'Except for his big sister,' said Tom hastily. 'She looks after him usually.'

He smiled inwardly at the thought of Kylie, Scott's fifteen-year-old sister, having anything more to do with Scott than she could possibly help. He gulped down the last of his tea and pushed his chair back.

'I'll just try, then. See if he's there,' he said, and bolted out of the room.

He dialled the familiar number with fingers that trembled in anticipation, then sat back, counting the rings. Five, six, seven. Scott couldn't have gone out already, could he? It was much too early in the morning. Nine, ten. His heart was sinking. He couldn't bear it, he just couldn't *bear* it, if Scott wasn't going to be there after all. Twelve, thirteen. He'd let it go on to fifteen rings, no, twenty, then he'd hang up and try again in case he'd got the wrong number.

On the sixteenth ring, someone at the other end picked up the receiver and a cross voice, thick with sleep, said, 'Who is it?'

'Is that you, Kylie?' said Tom, his own voice squeaky with excitement. 'Is Scott there?'

'Who's that?' Kylie said.

'It's me, Tom. Scott's friend.'

'Tom? What do you want to phone people up for at this time of day? It's practically the middle of the night.'

'No it's not. It's nine o'clock. Is Scott there? Please, Kylie.'

'Tom, did you say? I thought you'd gone off to live in Africa.'

'I have. I did. I've come back. Where's Scott?'

'Off on holiday. With Eddy. Won't be back till Sunday.'

Tom felt as if the floor was heaving under his feet.

'With Eddy? Eddy Fowler? But he doesn't even like Eddy!'

'You could have fooled me. Eddy practically lives here when Scott's not over at his place.'

Tom replaced the receiver and collapsed onto the overstuffed sofa as if he'd been knocked over. This was it. This was the end. His one hope, the one light in his dark night, had been snuffed out. Scott had deserted him. Scott had a new best friend, that creepy little nerd, Eddy Fowler, who used to follow him and Scott round and get in the way all the time and sneak off and tell tales and crawl up to teachers.

He couldn't move. He felt stuck to this horrible sofa as if he was being pressed down onto it with heavy weights.

Mrs Norris came in.

'All fixed up?' she said brightly. 'Did you get your friend?'

'No, he's away,' Tom said shortly.

He found he could stand up after all, and he pushed past her out of the room.

'I'm going to sort my things out,' he said, and fled upstairs.

He'd hardly opened his suitcase last night. He'd just tossed a few things out of it and pulled out his pyjamas and toothbrush. But the case was there now, on the floor, overflowing with his clothes. He supposed he'd have to unpack it some-time, but it certainly wouldn't be now.

He sat down on his bed. He was going to cry. He *had* to cry, and he didn't even care if anyone heard him.

No one did. After a while there didn't seem to be much point in crying any more. He wiped his eyes on his sleeve and blew his nose, then he knelt down and rummaged in his suitcase. There was a wildlife magazine somewhere, among all the sweaters and socks, that Afra had given him. He didn't read that kind of thing normally, but even flicking through it would remind him of her and Joseph. Of Africa.

Downstairs he heard the phone ring. A moment later, Mrs Norris called up, 'Tom, it's for you.'

Maybe it's Auntie Jean again, he thought hope-fully. Maybe she's going to come and see me.

He ran downstairs into the lounge and picked up the receiver.

'Tom? Is that you?'

It was Jas.

'Jas!' Tom was surprised by how pleased he was to hear her voice. 'How did you know my number?'

'I got it off those Norris people. What hap-pened yesterday? Did they get the guy?'

She'd dropped her scornful tone of voice and sounded eager and friendly. Tom responded with a rush of warmth.

'Oh Jas, it was so amazing. Yes, they got him, and the other guy.'

'What other guy?'

'Well, Sweatface, you know, our guy, he handed the bag on to someone else and—'

'Damn, Jinjy's woken up,' she interrupted him. 'Listen Tom, I've got to go. My sister's out shopping and I'm looking after the baby. Why don't you come round here this morning? I want to hear everything. All about it!'

Tom's heart lifted.

'Yes, I'd like that. You've no idea. Where are you?'

'It's a bit of a way but you can do it easily on the 37 bus, my sister says. She looked up where you are. She says you just go down to the end of your road and get on the 37 outside the police station. Get off at the big McDonald's next to the sofa factory. I'll meet you at the bus stop in about an hour. OK?'

'OK,' said Tom jubilantly.

He turned to see Mrs Norris in the doorway.

'Who was it?' she said.

'Jas.' Tom was suddenly cautious. 'It's the girl I came over on the plane with.'

Mrs Norris frowned.

'Her mum, Bibi, and my mum are practically best friends,' he went on glibly. 'Mum asked Jas to make sure she introduced me to her big sister before she went back. She's invited me over this morning.'

'Over? Where?'

'To Hounslow. It's not far. It's on the 37 bus route, Jas says. She's meeting me in an hour.'

'You can't just go off by yourself, on buses,' said Mrs Norris. 'You might get lost. Miss the stop. Anything. And I don't know these people. I'm responsible for you and if anything happens—'

'But I've fixed it with Jas,' said Tom. 'She'll be waiting for me at the bus stop.'

'Call her back, dear,' said Mrs Norris, turning to leave the room. 'Say you'll go over another time. I'll take you there myself one day.'

'She was calling from a payphone!' said Tom, inventing desperately. 'And she goes back to Kenya next week. She'll have her sister's baby with her. I can't just leave them there, waiting for me, not with the baby and all.'

'Let him go, Cynth,' said Mr Norris's voice from the other side of the door. 'He can't come to any harm. Take our phone number, Tom, and call us up if anything goes wrong. And don't talk to strangers, OK?'

Tom suppressed a gust of hysterical laughter.

'I won't,' he said.

He saw Jas from the bus before it pulled up at the stop, and he tumbled off it feeling as if he'd found his only friend in the world. She was pushing a stroller, and a tiny baby lay curled up in it, fast asleep, his long dark lashes sweeping his cheeks.

'He's sweet,' said Tom, looking at him briefly.

Jas straightened the baby's cover with a maternal flourish and they began to walk along the road.

'Tell me everything,' she said. 'I've been dying to hear.'

It was brilliant, telling the story to Jas. She gazed at Tom with open-mouthed respect when he explained how he'd jumped into Brown Hat's car. She exclaimed with shocked disgust when he described the trussed-up parrots. She shuddered at the emergence of the black mamba and doubled over with laughter when he told her about the hatching chicks.

'I just wish I'd been there!' she said, straightening up again. 'I wish I'd seen it all. What are they going to do with the parrots and the snakes and everything?'

'I don't know,' said Tom. 'Try to find good homes for them, Rob said. The worst part is that they can't just take them back to Africa and release them back into the wild. At least, maybe they could with the snakes, but not with the birds.'

'It's those poor parrots I'm thinking of,' said Jas. 'I mean, imagine if Sunny had been all tied up like that and packed off somewhere strange. He's so sensitive, he even gets upset when my friends get too noisy around him. He'd go crazy if he'd been treated like that.'

'I'd really, really like to see those parrots again, just to find out how they are,' said Tom. 'And Rob, too. He's so nice. You'd like him.'

'Well, why don't we?' said Jas. 'Heathrow's not that far away. Why don't we call your Norrises, and say you're staying with me for the day, and drop the baby back with my sister, and just go there and knock on the door?'

Tom stopped dead on the pavement, causing an old lady behind to almost bump into him.

'Jas, that's brilliant!' he said. 'Wait though. What if they don't let us in?'

'Oh they will. They will!' said Jas. 'You're the proper little hero, don't forget. If anyone's got the right to check up on those parrots, it's you!'

## 14

# FROGS, IGUANAS AND
# VULTURES' EGGS

Tom felt almost nervous as he pressed the buzzer by the front door of the Animal Reception Centre. The events of the day before seemed so incredible he almost wondered if he'd made them up. And if it had all been true, supposing Mr Stokes and Rob weren't there today, and there were people who didn't know him? They'd send him away with a few sharp words and he'd feel a fool in front of Jas.

His fears were fulfilled when a strange young woman opened the door.

'Is Rob here?' said Tom, crossing his fingers behind his back.

'I'll see,' the girl said repressively. 'Who are you?'

'Tom,' Tom said. 'I was here yesterday.'

'Oh, you're *the* Tom!' she said. 'I've heard all about you. Come on in.'

She opened the door into the animal holding section and called out, 'Rob, look who's here! The boy wonder!'

Rob came clumping out in his rubber boots, grinning broadly.

'I guessed we hadn't seen the last of you,' he said. 'And who's this?'

'Jas,' said Tom. 'She was with me on the plane. She's the one who spotted the parrot's feathers through the airhole.'

'Partners in crime-busting!' said Rob, laughing. 'I suppose you've got a whole gang of villains out there in the car park, and you've come to hand them over?'

'Yeah, course we have.' Tom felt as if he'd landed back in the real world after escaping from a foggy grey no-man's land. 'But first we thought, well, we wondered if we could see how the parrots and tortoises and everything were getting on.'

'Strictly against regulations,' Rob said cheer-fully, 'but regs are made to be broken. Actually, I hoped you'd be back. I wanted to tell you what else we found on that Sweatface of yours.'

'You mean you found more things?' Tom said eagerly. 'More animals?'

'Oh yes.' Rob handed them each an overall. 'We went through that black shoulder bag he was carrying. There was a camera bag in it, and some little film canisters. Five or six of them. I knew they'd have some odd inhabitants as soon as I saw the airholes drilled through the tops. True enough, there was a little Mantella frog from Madagascar in every one. A highly endangered species. And inside the camera case, instead of a camera, he'd got a baby iguana. Lively little fellow. When I opened the bag up he tried to take my finger off.'

'He's a monster, that man!' Jas said indignantly. 'They all might have died.'

'Two of the frogs had died,' said Rob. He was watching as they chose rubber boots from the rack, and tied masks round their faces. 'Are you ready? Right. In we go. There's more bad news first, though. The third parrot, the smallest one, didn't make it. I found him this morning on the floor of the cage. The shock, I expect. He was so listless yesterday I guessed he wouldn't survive.'

'But are the other two all right?' asked Tom anxiously.

'Not bad. One of them, the biggest, the first one we unwrapped, he's a little fighter. He's doing brilliantly. He's got personality, that bird. A class act. Deafened me with his squawking and whistling this morning.'

'And the other one?' said Jas. 'There were three, weren't there?'

'You'll see.'

Rob pushed open the door of a little room off the corridor. The parrots had been moved out of the surgery. They were in an aviary that took up more than half the room. One of them, the smaller of the two, was on the highest perch, standing on one leg. His head had been laid back in sleep, but it jerked up when the door opened and he gave a muted squawk, then cocked his head to look down at the intruders, dropping his other claw to the perch.

'Good sign, that he was standing on one leg,' said Rob softly. 'They only rest on two when they're poorly. He's got a good chance, if he doesn't develop a disease in the next couple of days.'

The other parrot was investigating the wire wall of the aviary. He was climbing up and down on it, using his handsome curved black beak and his speckled grey claws with extraordinary agility.

'He's looking for a way out,' Rob said.

The parrot stopped moving when he heard Rob's voice. With an outraged screech, he took off and fluttered onto the lower perch, showing off his magnificent flame tail feathers. He began sidling up and down along it, bobbing his head angrily.

'He's telling us to get lost,' Rob said. 'He's the boss man here. Proper little character, isn't he?'

Jas had approached the wire and was standing quietly, watching the birds. Then she made a low whistling sound. Both parrots stopped moving and stood, with their heads on one side, listening.

'Well done,' said Rob approvingly. 'You've got a way with them.'

'We've got an African grey at home,' Jas told him. 'He likes it when I make that noise. I do it when he gets upset. What's going to happen to these two?'

'Wish I knew. The customs people take over that part of it. It'll be a while before anything happens, I expect. The birds have to stay here for thirty-five days, in quarantine, to make sure they don't develop any nasties.'

'I'd just so like to take them home!' Jas said, with quiet vehemence. 'To put them with Sunny!'

'Sunny's got this huge, brilliant aviary in Nairobi,' Tom told Rob. 'It'd be a million times better than anything they'd get here.'

'Sunny mightn't like it though.' Rob looked dubious. 'He mightn't want a couple of house-mates.'

'I know *that*!' Jas was scornful again. 'You have to introduce them slowly, put them alongside each other in separate cages for a while. They tell you how to do it at KSPCA.'

Rob was turning away.

'Don't you want to see the snakes, and the chicks, and the tortoises?' he said.

The snakes were in the next room, in a series of glass tanks lining the walls.

'Interesting little collection,' said Rob, peering through the glass front of the nearest tank. 'Most of the snakes were Angolan pythons, very endangered, that the guy was presumably trying to pass off as the less rare pythons. He'd have succeeded a few years ago. Pity no one told him that we've sharpened up our procedures. Tight as a ball of string it is here now. Still, we'd have missed everything else except the pythons, probably, if you hadn't alerted us.'

'What'll happen to him now?' said Tom.

'Prison, I expect,' Rob answered with satisfaction. 'The punishment really fits the crime in this case, as he was sending all these creatures into captivity. Kind captivity, if their new owners were kind, but captivity all the same.'

'He won't be able to do it again for a while,' said Tom.

Rob glanced down at him.

'No. Your Sweatface is out of action now. But he's only a little fish, I'm afraid. The big guys running this thing will get other couriers, trying new tricks. We have to go on keeping a step ahead.'

Jas was looking with horrible fascination at a small snake in a glass tank, which was coiling and uncoiling itself in a sinuous dance.

'A Madagascar tree boa,' said Rob. 'One of the rarest snakes in the world. Pretty little thing, isn't it?'

Tom glanced at Rob, wondering if he was being funny, but Rob was smiling down at the young snake with fond admiration. 'Pretty' wasn't a word Tom would have used himself, but he could see, now he came to look more closely, that the delicate little creature's shining scales and rippling folds, if not pretty exactly, were beautiful, in a way.

Jas hadn't moved from the door.

'Sorry,' she said, 'but I really, really can't do snakes. They just give me the horrors. I keep thinking one's got out and it's climbing up my leg.'

Tom looked down at his own legs with an involuntarily shudder. Rob's enthusiasm had started to infect him, but the snakes still made him nervous. He followed the others out of the room with relief.

'Now this, you're going to love,' said Rob, opening the door into the next room.

They spent no more than a moment, looking in at a small glass tank where several little tree frogs were barely visible among the bright green leaves of a bush, because at the far end of the room stood an incubator, its base covered with soft chippings, and staggering round in it, their brand new feathers still clinging wetly to their skins, were a couple of freshly hatched baby birds. Three more, their down fluffed out with all the maturity of one-day-old hatchlings, were cheeping furiously, stimulated by the movement in the room as if they were in their own nest, and were trying to attract the attention of a parent returning from the hunt. Lying embedded in the chips lay seven or eight other large white and speckled eggs.

'In an ideal world,' Rob said, 'I'd use bird puppets to feed them with, so they wouldn't become fixated on my human hands, but it's hard to tell what species these little guys are. There are at least four baby vultures here, and a couple of eagles. Not sure, yet, if they're Martial or Bateleur, but you've only got to look at those beaks to see that they'll be fearsome when they're big boys.'

The chicks had rushed to the edge of the incubator, cheeping furiously, their mouths gaping wide open.

'OK,' said Rob. 'Time for the next meal.'

He took the cover off a bowl beside the incubator to reveal a plateful of chopped meat.

'With the tweezers,' he said to Tom. 'Poke the food right down their throats, like their mums would. Have a go.'

'I've done this before,' said Tom, remembering how he'd fed caterpillars once to Jonathan Swift, a baby bird that Afra had rescued.

He wasn't prepared, though, for the powerful greed of these miniature birds of prey. They jostled each other out of the way, their mouths stretched wide open, little pink caverns of hunger, and it was hard to believe that such piercing, raucous cries could come from such soft little frames.

'That's enough,' Rob said at last, 'even for baby

vultures. Now look over there. You haven't seen the tortoises yet.'

There were four tortoises altogether. Two were basking under the warm light of an incubator lamp, but the other two had squeezed themselves into a low-roofed box at the side of the tank.

'That's what these soft-shelled tortoises like to do,' said Rob. 'They get into a crevice and then, if a predator comes along and tries to winkle them out, they blow themselves up so they can't be dislodged.'

'That's brilliant,' said Jas admiringly. 'Where do they come from?'

'Anywhere in East Africa. Waller probably paid guys to go out and buy them off country people. Just think, tortoises would all be left in peace, where they belong, if people in Europe didn't fancy them as pets, and make a whole crazy trade out of living creatures. Do you realize that after drugs and guns, smuggling endangered animals and their products is the biggest illegal trade in the world? The rarer the creatures, the more people will pay. Thousands and thousands of pounds, sometimes.'

'How do they buy them?' asked Jas. 'I mean, you can't just walk into a pet shop and buy an animal that's been smuggled here from Africa, can you?'

'Yes, sometimes.' Rob was scowling. 'Not all pet shop owners are honest. Some of them make a killing out of animals caught in the wild. And do the people who go in to buy them bother to ask where they've come from? Like hell they do. Sick, isn't it?'

'Sick's right,' nodded Tom, peering closely at the little tortoises. 'How did you get all those horrible screws out of them? Did it hurt them?'

'Hard to tell with tortoises.' Rob was leaning over the incubator, gazing happily at the little creatures. 'I think they'll do all right now though.'

'I just don't understand why you can't send them back to where they came from,' said Tom. 'I mean, if you don't, it sort of means that the smugglers have won, doesn't it?'

'But we don't know where they did come from.'

'Yes you do. You said just now. East Africa.'

'East Africa's a big place. Their home territory was probably a few hundred metres square. They'll have known every square inch of it, they'll have learned every little rock and bush and dip in the ground since they hatched out of their eggs. They'll know every food source, every hiding place, every kind of danger. If you put them down somewhere else, even a mile away from their old home, they'd be confused and lost, and anything hungry could just snap them up. Anyway, if there were other, resident tortoises there, they'd chase them off their patch.'

'OK,' said Jas. 'Yeah, OK. I see that. It would be like if I said I was from Kenya, and someone just dumped me down in the middle of nowhere, in Tsavo National Park or something. I'd be eaten by lions, probably. Dead meat in twenty-four hours.'

'I wouldn't mind,' Tom burst out. The last hour, with Rob, had been brilliant. He'd been able to push his awful situation out of his mind, but the realization of it had suddenly flooded over him again. 'I wouldn't mind even being dumped in the middle of a gamepark just so long I was in Kenya again. I'd find my way out of it, and get myself back home again and—'

He didn't want to go on in case he embarrassed himself by crying.

Rob looked at him curiously.

'What are you doing in England, anyway?' he said. 'I didn't quite get it yesterday. I wondered, after you'd gone.'

'I'm supposed to be going to some stupid school here,' said Tom bitterly. 'For my own good.'

'Oh. Those people who fetched you, are they your grandparents?'

'No!' exploded Tom, startling the vulture and eagle chicks, who started cheeping again. 'I'd never seen them before in my life. I'm supposed to be living with them at the weekends, and I just can't *bear* it. They're trying to be nice to me, I know they are, but they just haven't got any idea. They're – oh, I can't explain it!'

'You don't need to,' said Rob. 'They didn't look a whole lot of laughs to me.'

'I'll tell your mum and dad, when I go home next week,' Jas said. 'I'll tell them you're really unhappy, and you shouldn't have to stay there.'

'Why bother?' Tom shook his head. 'It won't do any good. I just feel like – oh, like those chicks, and the parrots and everything. I'm stuck. I can't go back.'

'But haven't you got a return ticket?' asked Rob.

'Yes, but I'm not allowed to use it till the end of term.'

'When I was your age,' said Rob, looking out of the window at the clouds scudding across the blue sky, 'I was always doing things I wasn't allowed to. It got me into a lot of trouble, but I kind of didn't like being pushed around. I still don't.'

'What do you mean?' Tom was staring at him, his attention caught.

'Mean? I don't mean anything,' said Rob, still not looking at him. 'But if I had a ticket that would take me home—'

He stopped.

'You'd use it,' said Tom. He felt breathless suddenly.

'Oh, I didn't say that,' Rob said. 'I don't know what I'd do. Now look, you kids, I've got work to do. You'd better push off. Hang up your overalls on the way out.'

# 15

# A DESPERATE PLAN

'You wouldn't though, would you?' said Jas, as she and Tom walked slowly away from the Animal Reception Centre. 'Just go home on your own, I mean?' Tom didn't say anything. He was thinking.

There was a screaming roar overhead and they looked up to see the white body of a huge aeroplane fly up into the sky from the runway nearby. Tom watched it as it rose, like a great metal arrow, and grew rapidly smaller and smaller, curving round in a wide circle to head for the south. He could be inside that thing himself. He could be one of those people, looking out of one of those tiny windows. He could be going home.

'I don't know,' he said, 'I don't know if I've got the guts.'

'You? No guts?' She snorted. 'You're the boy who chased after a smuggler, and jumped into a stranger's car, and persuaded a whole lot of customs guys to arrest him.'

'It would take more than that,' he said, 'to face my mum and dad. They'd go totally, totally mad. Up the wall. Out of the window.'

'It's your life,' said Jas, shrugging.

They walked side by side down the pavement towards the bus stop. I've got a choice, Tom kept repeating in his head. If I want to go badly enough, I can.

'It's the sad old smell I can't stand,' he said suddenly.

'What smell?' said Jas. 'What are you talking about?'

'The Norrises. It's like they haven't opened the window for years and years.'

'Oh.'

'And they had a little girl called Bethany, who died, and they don't know any kids my age. They think cold rice pudding's a treat and that I ought to go to bed at eight o'clock. And I don't reckon they've ever even heard of pizza.'

'Mm.'

'It's not that they're cruel or anything. It's just that they're . . .'

'Sad?'

'Yes, sad, and I can't stand it.'

'I thought you had a good friend you wanted to see?'

'I did, Scott. He's got another best mate now.'

The bus came. They got onto it and sat down.

'The school might be good though,' Jas said encouragingly.

'Or it might not,' said Tom. 'Anyway, I can't see what's wrong with the school in Nairobi. It's brilliant. Loads of people get fantastic exam results there.'

Jas smirked.

'You did, didn't you?' said Tom, looking up at her.

'Yes.' Jas tossed her plait back with a triumphant flick. 'I got a scholarship to my next school, the one I'm at now.'

'There you are then.'

Tom had brightened a little, but his gloom descended again.

'If my dad wasn't planning to go off to South Africa, I wouldn't have to start at this new place in the middle of term. That's the bit I'm dreading. Everybody'll have their friends all set up already.'

'What's it called, this school?' said Jas.

'Uplands Grove,' said Tom sarcastically. 'What a stupid name for a school.'

Jas looked at him, surprised.

'Uplands Grove?' she said. 'My brother-in-law was talking about that place this morning. They were trying to decide where to send Jinjy.'

'Who's Jinjy?'

'My nephew, Gurjinder.'

'Your nephew? That little baby?' said Tom. 'But he's only just been born!'

'That doesn't matter. They've got his whole career planned out already. He's going to play cricket for England, be the first man to set foot on Mars and be the first Asian Prime Minister, at the same time as having a brilliant career as a heart surgeon and a university professor and a judge, as far as I can make out.'

'Yeah,' said Tom, 'and all he'll want to do is mess about and play computer games. So what did they say about Uplands Grove anyway?'

'They said they wouldn't send him there because of some scandal or other.'

'What scandal?' Tom was listening eagerly. 'Was it sex? Molesting kids or something? That'd be brilliant. They'd even close the school down for that.'

'Not paedophiles,' said Jas, wrinkling her forehead, 'but there was something about sex.'

'What? Come on Jas, you must remember!'

'Oh yes,' Jas's brow cleared. 'It was the headmaster. He had an affair with the school secretary and ran off with all the money. The school's broke. Loads of kids have been leaving. There was a whole lot about it in the local papers a while ago.'

'Wow, that's just amazing!'

They'd reached the stop now, and Tom was following Jas off the bus.

'They couldn't still want me to go to a school with a sex-crazed headteacher and not enough money to pay for our food or the pencils and paper and stuff, could they?'

'No – no, I suppose not. Wait a minute, have I

got it right? Was it Uplands Grove, or was it Parkview Place?'

Tom grabbed her arm.

'Jas, you've got to remember. You just must!'

She shook him off.

'OK, don't get in a state. I'll ask my sister tonight. She'll know.'

'Tonight? That'll be too late,' said Tom. 'I've got to go to the school tomorrow. Once they've got me, they might just kind of keep me. I won't know how to get away.'

They were walking past a parade of shops. Jas gave a sudden exclamation and walked into one of them.

'Hang on a minute,' she said. 'I've just thought of something.'

She came back a moment later with a newspaper in her hand.

'It's in here,' she said. 'My sister was reading this paper this morning. It's got that thing about the school in it.'

Tom almost grabbed it out of her hands.

'Let's see,' he said. 'Where is it?'

The news piece was on page two, under a headline that read 'Local School in Fraud Scandal. Head Quits'.

The words danced in front of Tom's eyes as he looked down at the page, but he forced himself to read slowly enough to take them in.

'Uplands Grove, a local private school, was

rocked with scandal at the weekend as head-master, Charles Trim (52) absconded with £250,000 in cash, the pre-paid fees of the second half of term. The school secretary, Ms Jeanette Bowler (41), has also disappeared and is believed to have joined Mr Trim at a secret destination abroad. The school governors issued a statement last evening endorsing their support for the school.

"It's business as usual," Col. Gerry Fairweather, the chairman of the governors told this news-paper. "Uplands Grove is an excellent school and we will make sure that none of our pupils suffer." Several parents have already removed their children from the exclusive school and more are expected to follow.'

Tom looked up, his eyes shining.

'Jas,' he said 'You're . . . you're . . .' He was about to say 'an angel', but thought better of it. 'Brilliant,' he finished lamely.

'It's not me.' She was walking on down the pavement. 'You'd better thank my sister.'

'You'll have to thank her for me,' said Tom, 'I won't have time.'

'Why not?'

He took a deep breath.

'Because I'm going to be on the next flight to Nairobi, that's why not!'

*

It was nearly 5 o'clock when he arrived back at the Norrises' house. Mrs Norris answered the door.

'Oh Tom,' she said. 'Come in quietly. Uncle's asleep. Did you have a nice time with – what's her name, your friend?'

'Jas – yes thanks,' said Tom politely. He felt sorry for Mrs Norris, now that he knew what he was going to do.

Mrs Norris stepped back to let him come in.

'You've been out a long time,' she said, reproof in her voice.

'Yes, we . . .' Tom thought rapidly. 'We had to take the baby for a walk. To the park. We fed the ducks.'

Mrs Norris's face softened at the mention of the baby.

'A baby?' she said. 'That's nice. Now you get along up to your room. I've unpacked your suitcase for you and put it away, up in the attic. You'll find all your things in the drawers. Let's try and keep our things nice and tidy from now on, shall we?'

Tom looked at her in dismay. He'd counted on his suitcase still being almost ready to zip up and carry down the stairs. He didn't have a clear plan in his head yet, but the adrenalin was pumping round his veins. He was filled with an odd sense of confidence, sure that things would somehow fall into place. He pulled himself together and put on a smile.

'I'll go up then,' he said.

His room was uncomfortably tidy. He opened one drawer after the other in the chest by the window. His socks, pyjamas, sweatshirts and trousers were folded and put away with alarming neatness.

My passport! he thought, with a shock of alarm. My ticket! Where are they?

They'd been in his hand baggage the night before, in the bag he'd carried on his shoulder. The bag was right there, lying behind the chair where it had fallen last night. By a miracle, she hadn't found it.

He knelt down on the floor, ripped open the velcro flap of the front pocket and heaved a sigh of relief. His passport and ticket were still in the same place. And so was the rest of the English money that Simon had given him. It wasn't a huge amount, but it would be enough to get him to the airport.

He rocked back on his heels, thinking furiously. Planes went late at night to Nairobi, he knew that. He could get on one tonight, if he left before eight o'clock. He smiled.

Early to bed, he whispered to himself. That'll please them, anyway.

He could only take a little bit of luggage with him, just one or two things he'd really need on the journey. The rest of the stuff would have to be sent back to Nairobi somehow.

Jas! He thought, with a flash of inspiration. Her case had been full of baby stuff on the way to London. She could fill it up on the way back with Tom's things.

Mrs Norris had done him a favour after all. It would have been impossible to get his heavy case out of his room, down the creaking stairs, and out of the house without being detected.

Quickly, he stuffed into his little rucksack the book his dad had given him, his toothbrush, the piece of paper with Jas's phone number on it and, at the last moment, the newspaper with the piece about Uplands Grove School.

Now for the note, he thought. I'll have to write them a note.

He tore a piece of paper out of the little notebook he'd had with him on the plane and sat, chewing the end of his biro, wondering what to say. He didn't want to upset the Norrises. They'd meant well, he knew.

At last he wrote,

Dear Mr and Mrs Norris,
(He couldn't bring himself to write Uncle and Auntie) I'm very sorry to be rude and not say goodbye, but I know things aren't going to work out for me here. The school's all in a mess and the headmaster's run off with the money. It's all

in the local paper. I'm going home tonight, on the plane, and you musn't worry because I've flown loads of times before and I know exactly what to do. I'll get Mum to call you from Nairobi.

Thanks a lot for having me. It was really kind of you to think about taking me fishing.

Tom

He finished the note and stuffed it under his pillow. It wasn't perfect but it would have to do. He'd leave it on his pillow when he left, and Mrs Norris would find it there in the morning. He ran downstairs and into the kitchen.

'Mrs Norris, I mean Auntie,' he said. 'Do you mind if I have supper early tonight? I'm really tired. It must be jetlag or something. I'd sort of like to be in bed by seven.'

# 16

# SNAKES AND LADDERS

Tonight's supper was even worse than last night's.

'Lamb stew,' said Mrs Norris triumphantly, doling out onto Tom's plate a glutinous mass of meat and pale vegetables.

Tom, who had felt guilty the minute he'd walked into the kitchen and seen Mrs Norris by the cooker, felt his resolve harden again. If he stayed, he'd have to face her cooking every weekend, and he'd probably starve to death.

He forced himself to eat the whole plateful, the knowledge that he'd never have to eat another meal in this house again giving him the necessary courage.

He was eating alone again this evening. Mrs Norris saw him glance at the rest of the empty table and said, 'Uncle and I are going to have ours while we watch "Star Struck". We always watch "Star Struck" on a Friday. It doesn't start till half-past seven.'

She took his plate away and plonked down in front of him a bowlful of bright green jelly. Tom closed his eyes for a brief moment, willing the shivering green stuff to go away, but he knew he had no choice. He lifted his spoon, smiled bravely and gulped the whole lot down.

'More?' said Mrs Norris, waiting, spoon in hand, to tip another revolting mound into his bowl.

'No thanks,' said Tom hastily. He yawned theatrically. 'I'll be off to bed then. Goodnight.'

He slipped off his chair and made for the door.

'I'll come up later and see you're all right,' said Mrs Norris.

His heart missed a beat.

'No, no! I mean, please don't,' he said. 'I don't sleep very well at the beginning of the night, and if something wakes me up I can't go off again.'

She looked at him, surprised, and for a moment he was afraid he'd made her suspicious. Then she smiled.

'I know how you feel. I toss and turn all night if I get disturbed first thing.'

He couldn't look at her. He was going to feel bad enough about how worried and upset they'd be. He didn't want his last sight of her to be her anxious, well-meaning smile.

'Goodnight then,' he mumbled, and went out of the kitchen.

Once in his room, he checked his bag and put on his jacket, then sat down on the narrow bed to wait. It was just after seven o'clock. There was nothing he could do till they were settled in the lounge in front of the TV.

He considered his options. There was no point in trying to climb out of the window. The drop down to the patio below was a sheer five metres, and he'd break a leg or something, besides making a thud that would bring them running to find out what had happened. He could slip out of the back door, of course, but there'd be no access to the road from there. He'd be trapped in a network of little back gardens.

No, his only real choice was to go out the way he'd come in, through the front, right past the door of the lounge, where Mr and Mrs Norris would be sitting, their supper trays on their knees. His heart was pounding already at the thought of it.

He looked at his watch. A quarter past seven. Both the Norrises were in the kitchen now. He could hear them moving around. Doors were opening and closing and something was beginning to squeak. He frowned, trying to work it out, and remembered an old trolley under a workbench in the kitchen. Mrs Norris had moved it at breakfast time, and its wheels had squeaked then.

He tried to imagine what they were doing. They must have loaded their revolting lamb stew onto the trolley, and were wheeling it down to the lounge. This was the moment then! Before they'd settled down quietly into their chairs, this was his chance to get away!

He opened his bedroom door. He could hear

them in the lounge, fussing around, switching on lamps and fiddling with the heater. He crept to the top of the stairs. A shaft of light was coming out through the lounge door. They hadn't closed it then. He gave a tiny grunt of disappointment. He couldn't possibly risk it, he wouldn't dare to creep past an open door. The floorboards might creak, and anyway, the click of the front door opening and closing would certainly give him away.

He was standing in an agony of indecision when he heard Mr Norris say clearly, as though he was right by the open lounge door, 'Don't worry, Cynth. I'll get it.'

He froze. He could see the lounge door opening, and Mr Norris coming out. From up here the light shone on his bald patch. If he looked up, he'd be sure to see Tom, standing at the top of the stairs, his incriminating rucksack in his hand, and his outdoor jacket on. Tom's heart was pounding in his chest as loud as an amplified drum kit.

Mr Norris went on into the kitchen and came back a moment later with a glass in his hand, then he hesitated at the bottom of the stairs and went back towards the kitchen again.

'Come on, Paul! It's starting!' Mrs Norris called out.

'Coming dear,' Mr Norris called back. 'Just getting the salt.'

He came hurrying back down the hall again, went into the lounge and shut the door with a click behind him.

Tom felt the adrenalin rush up through his body and he obeyed it. He flew down the stairs on silent feet, crept past the lounge door and opened the front door. Then he held it almost shut, waiting for a burst of sound from the television that would cover the click of the closing door. The signature tune of the programme was still playing, rising to a crescendo. It was now or never. With a silent prayer, he pulled the door shut behind him.

The click seemed deafening. He darted down the short path to the street and stood for a moment, watching and waiting, but there was no movement from inside the house.

Suddenly, he felt horribly alone. The house looked less dingy than it had done yesterday, the light streaming through the crack between the living room curtains almost warm and welcoming. He could be in there now, on the sofa, watching TV in the warmth and light. He was almost tempted to walk back up the path, knock on the door, and be let back in.

Then he thought of what they'd say to him, of how impossible it would be to explain, and he knew it was already too late. He turned his back on the house and began to run down the street towards the main road.

*

The bright lights of Terminal Three almost dazzled him when he stepped into the departures hall. The journey had been easier than he'd expected. He'd taken the 37 bus again, and asked the driver how to get to the terminals at Heathrow Airport. He'd only had to change buses once, and the second one had come along quite quickly.

He realized though, looking down the concourse, that the hardest bit was still to come. He had to actually get himself onto the plane. He had to find out when the next one to Nairobi left, and book a seat, and think up a good story that would account not only for why he was travelling unaccompanied, but also why he'd arrived at the airport completely on his own.

His mind was working fast and with unusual clarity. He was thinking ahead, imagining what could go wrong, and planning for it.

Information was the first thing he needed, and there, ahead of him, just as he was wondering where to go, was a desk marked 'Information'.

'Excuse me,' he said to the bored girl behind it. 'When's the next flight to Nairobi? I'm supposed to be seeing some friends off, but they didn't tell me exactly what time the plane leaves.'

Her eyes were on her computer terminal. She hardly looked up.

'Which airline?'

Tom's fingers were crossed tightly behind his back.

'Kenya Airways.'

She tapped something else into her terminal.

'Kenya Airways,' she repeated at last. 'Departure 22.55 from this terminal. It's not up on the departure board yet. You're too early.'

He was already walking away. He wanted to punch the air with his fist. He was up the first rung of the ladder. There was a flight tonight, and he was in time for it.

He forced himself to stay calm. There were many more rungs, slippery ones too, to climb before he was safe. He grinned wryly. And some snakes to slide down as well, probably.

Booking a seat, that's the next thing, he muttered.

He looked round. The departures hall was huge, and very confusing. Thousands of people were milling around, pushing their trolleys towards the check-in desks, above which were the brightly lit names of a host of different airlines.

Gulf Air, Indian Airlines, Cathay Pacific, he read. But where was Kenya Airways?

Then he saw the familiar red and white sign. No one was queuing at it yet, but a couple of uniformed girls were already sitting waiting behind their desks. He wanted to run towards them, feeling that he only had to present himself and they'd be sure to scoop him up and take him home. He stopped himself in time.

Don't blow it. Get it right, he told himself sternly. Don't rush things.

He was about to walk up to the check-in desk and try his luck, when another sign on the crowded concourse leaped out at him.

'Ticket Sales and Reservations', it said.

He hesitated. Perhaps it would be better, after all, to try to book a seat first. Then at least he'd have something definite to go on.

There was a short queue under the sign. He joined it, and took his ticket out of his bag. A moment later, he was in front of a smartly uniformed young man.

'Yes?' the young man said, looking over Tom's shoulder, obviously expecting an adult to appear. Tom gave him what he hoped was a winsome smile. He felt inspired.

'My auntie sent me over,' he said. 'She's in the toilet with my cousin. He's got diarrhoea.'

An expression of distaste crossed the young man's face.

'I've got to go to Nairobi tonight,' Tom went on, 'because my mum's there, and she—' he hesitated, afraid that the lie he was about to tell might bring real bad luck. 'She's really ill. She's had an accident. In a car.'

The young man looked sympathetic, and held out his hand for Tom's ticket.

'Travelling on your own, are you? Have you done it before?'

'Oh yes. Loads of times.' Tom's palms were sweating, but he was breathing more easily. Something told him that this was going to work.

The man checked his ticket, then began to tap something out on his terminal.

'You're in luck,' he said, smiling up at Tom. 'I can get you on flight KQ101, departing tonight at 22.55. Only three seats left on the whole plane.'

'Fantastic,' said Tom. He had to work to keep the grin off his face. He'd told the guy his mum had been in an accident. He ought to be looking upset.

The man handed the ticket back to him.

'You'll have to get your aunt to go to the check-in desk with you,' he said. 'They'll need confirmation that it's all OK and above board. Oh yes, and they'll want to call your family in Nairobi too, to make sure they know when you'll be arriving, and can pick you up at the airport.'

Tom stared at him, the colour draining from his face.

'Oh right. Thanks,' he managed to say, and walked away on legs that suddenly felt stiff.

He sank down onto a nearby empty seat, and despair flooded over him.

It would be impossible, after all. He ought to have known things would go wrong. It had been mad, totally crazy, to imagine he could just run away, and fly home, all on his own.

What do I do now? he thought. I can't just go back to the Norrises. I won't!

His mind felt numb. He didn't know whether to stay sitting where he was, or to run up to someone, anyone, and ask for help, or to just walk out of the terminal and go off into the night.

A large woman, her sari fluttering, sank down onto the chair beside him with a gusty sigh of relief. She turned to the man following her and said something in an Indian language.

Jas! Tom thought. His mind was alert again. He had the beginnings of a plan.

He looked round. There were some telephone booths nearby. He hurried up to one, pushed some coins into the slot and dialled Jas's number.

She answered almost immediately.

'Jas,' he said, not letting her speak. 'You've got to help me. I'm at Heathrow, and I'm booked on a flight around eleven o'clock, but they won't let me get on it if someone doesn't say it's OK, like a grown-up relative or something.'

There was a moment's silence, then Jas said crisply, 'Are you asking me to pretend to be your relative?'

'Yes,' said Tom, holding his breath.

'OK.' Jas's voice sounded quite normal, as if she impersonated people every day of the week.

Tom felt a wonderful warmth creeping back through his veins.

'Give them my number,' Jas went on. 'Tell them

to ask for – wait a minute, it can't be Jaswant Singh because you're not Asian so I can't be your aunt.'

'Mrs Singer,' suggested Tom.

Jas giggled.

'Bit young to be your married aunt, aren't I? I won't be fifteen till January.'

'But you'll do it, won't you?' said Tom anxiously.

'Oh yes. I'd like to.' She put on a grown-up voice. 'Yes, of course I know Tom Wilkinson. I'd have brought him to the airport myself, except that I've broken my leg. Fell down the stairs while escaping from my husband. He's an axe murderer, you know.'

'Jas, please!'

She reverted to her usual voice.

'Don't worry, Tom. I'll do it. I'll enjoy it, actually.'

'Listen, don't hang up yet. There's another thing.'

'What? You want me to impersonate your uncle, too?'

'*Listen*. They're going to call Mum and Dad in Nairobi, to tell them to meet me.'

There was silence again at the other end. Tom fed another coin into the slot.

'Your mum and dad'll find out tomorrow, when you get back, anyway,' Jas said at last. 'But OK. If the airline does phone, I'll try and put them off. I'll tell them all the lines to Nairobi are busy, or something. I tell you what, though, my mum said she'd phone us this evening. When the phone rang, I thought it was her. I'll tell her to tell your parents you're on the plane, and she can kind of prepare them a bit, say you've been really miserable, and the school's a mess and everything. By the time you get home, they won't be too furious, with a bit of luck. Give me a bit of time, though. You don't have to check in just yet, do you?'

'Not for another hour,' said Tom. He felt almost giddy with relief. 'Jas, I don't know what to say. I—'

'It's OK.' Her voice was as cool as ever. 'And hey, good luck.'

By the time Tom had got back to the check-in desk, a queue was beginning to form. He looked round at the other travellers, hoping to see a family that he could casually attach himself to, like he'd done at the car park yesterday, but most of them were men, businessmen from the look of them, apart from a crowd of backpackers, who looked as if they were on a package tour.

The queue inched forward, then suddenly melted away altogether, and Tom found himself at the counter, passing his passport and ticket across to a bored girl in a Kenya Airways uniform, who took them from him almost without glancing up at him.

She processed his ticket automatically, and was about to hand it back to him when she seemed to become properly aware of him for the first time.

'No luggage?' she said.

Tom gulped. He hadn't thought of this one.

'My friend's mum went back to Kenya yesterday,' he said, inventing furiously. 'She took all my stuff with her.'

The girl looked suspicious.

'You're not on your own, are you?'

Tom tried to smile ingratiatingly.

'Yes, but it's all right.' A pulse was hammering in his throat. 'My aunt should have brought me, but she couldn't because she's ill. Here's her number if you want to call her. Her name's Mrs Singer.'

He pushed the piece of paper with Jas's number on it across the desk. The girl picked it up.

'You're a cool one,' she said admiringly. 'Wait here. I'll get someone to come and sort you out.'

'Oh it's OK,' Tom said quickly. 'I've flown alone loads of times before. I know how to get to the gate and everything. Anyway, I need to go to the toilet.'

She nodded.

'OK then. If you're sure you can manage. I'll get a call through to your aunt, and make sure someone meets you at the gate. You don't want to get on the wrong plane, do you?'

'No,' said Tom, ignoring her patronizing tone, and almost gasping with relief. 'Honestly, don't worry about me. I go to boarding school here. I have to go back to Nairobi on my own all the time. Done it for years. Sorry, I've really got to run.'

He darted away from the desk clutching the precious boarding card in his hand.

I've done it! I did it! he said to himself again and again. It'll be OK now. It's got to be OK now!

The next hour and a half seemed like a year. Making himself look as relaxed as possible, Tom got himself through passport control and the security check, then he found himself a seat in the departure lounge, sticking close to a couple of families with kids a bit younger than himself. He looked around him, trying to appear bored, whistling from time to time casually under his breath, anxious that at any moment a hand might fall on his shoulder, and an officious adult force him to hand over his boarding card and bundle him back to the Norrises. But nothing happened. No one looked at him.

At last his flight number and the number of the gate flashed up on the screen above his head. He had to restrain himself from jumping up and running to the gate, but he controlled himself and walked with admirable leisureliness down the endless corridors, and no one, except for the girl at the gate, who asked him with a smile if he was OK, spoke a word to him.

He walked onto the plane at last, his brain in a turmoil of triumph.

Home! I'm going home! Back to Africa! he kept thinking. And if Dad tries to send me back to England, I'll just do all this again. I'll just fly straight home again.

He found his seat and sat down, flexing the muscles of his arms, and feeling stronger and braver than he'd ever felt in his whole life before.

# 17

# GULLIVER

Tom had felt as light as a bird when the plane had taken off, roaring down the runway at Heathrow with glorious momentum. He'd even managed to sleep away an hour or two of the long night. But now that the plane was coming into land, floating down between a few puffy white clouds onto the hot tarmac of Jomo Kenyatta airport in Nairobi, his stomach was churning with dread.

They'll just go totally, totally mad with me, he kept thinking. Or they might be all sad and disappointed, and that would be even worse.

He stayed in his seat until everyone else had left the plane, reluctantly following the last passenger down the steps onto the tarmac. He didn't even bother to look up and savour the acres of golden grass beside the runway, and the blue sky of early morning above.

Maybe it was sort of cowardly, just running away like that, he thought. Maybe I should have stuck it out. Everyone else'll probably think so, anyway.

He reached the bottom of the steps. An airport official in a dazzling white shirt stepped forward.

'Tom Wilkinson?' he said. '*Kwaheri*. Welcome to Kenya. We have been waiting for you.'

Tom's heart skipped with fright. What could the man mean? Who could be waiting for him? How did anyone know he was here? Was this a trick of some kind? Had the smugglers somehow put a tail on him?

'Come with me,' the man said, smiling.

Warily, Tom followed him inside the double doors and into the airport building. If the guy tried to take him off into a side room or anything, he'd dodge away, lose himself in the crowd, get himself through passport control, then—

'Tom! Oh, Tom! Over here! It's me, Mum!'

Tom craned his neck, trying to see above the mass of passengers, and caught a glimpse of his mum and dad, forging their way through towards him. He stood still, setting his teeth.

Debbie reached him first and put her arms round him, almost crushing him in a violent hug.

'Oh Tom, I've been so worried about you. Are you all right? We tried and tried to call you at the Norrises but we couldn't get through.'

He hugged her back, his head in a whirl, then detached himself.

'I'm fine, Mum. How did you know I was here?'

'Bibi called last night, and then soon after the

phone began ringing again, and it's been on and on since first thing this morning.'

Tom didn't take in what she was saying. He was looking at his father. Simon had been talking to the white-shirted official, but now he turned towards Tom, and to his immense relief Tom saw that he was smiling.

'It's going to be in the VIP lounge,' he said to Debbie.

Tom looked him in the eye, screwing up his courage.

'Dad,' he said, 'I'm sorry. I really am. I was thinking on the plane, maybe I should have stuck it out.'

He stopped, as a memory came washing over him, of the Norrises at home, and the piece of cold tongue, and the desolation and desperation he had felt.

Simon shook his shoulder roughly.

'No, don't worry, son. Jean's been on the phone a few times. She said as soon as she heard your voice, when you'd arrived at the Norrises', she realized she'd made a terrible mistake. She hadn't thought it through. She'd kind of assumed that because they'd lost their little girl years ago, they'd be longing to have a kid in the house again, but she hadn't really worked out what it would be like for you. Typical Jean. Act first, think later. Pity it took her so long. And then Bibi's been on the phone non-stop too, with stuff about Uplands

Grove. Sounds as if it wasn't such a great place after all.' He smiled wryly. 'I suppose I got a bit carried away. The way Uplands Grove looked in the prospectus, you'd have thought it was Eton or something.'

'Do you mean I can stay here, at home?' said Tom. 'Have you asked Afra? I know they'd have me. I mean, if we offered to pay them for my food and stuff.'

'No need, old son,' said Simon. 'The South African contract's fallen through. I heard last night. Murchisons are still promoting me but they're keeping me here after all. You're going to be at home, with us.'

Tom felt as if it was his birthday and Christmas all rolled into one glorious moment. There was only one more thing he needed to find out.

'Do the Norrises know yet?' he asked guiltily. 'I crept out last night while they were watching telly. It's only seven o'clock in the morning in Britain, and they'll think I'm still asleep.'

'It's OK. I called them an hour ago,' Debbie said. 'They were a bit shocked of course. Said they couldn't understand why you hadn't told them you were so unhappy. Why didn't you, love?'

Tom shuddered.

'I just couldn't, that's all. You'd know if you'd met them.'

'Oh darling, was it that bad?' Debbie looked

upset. 'If we'd realized they were going to be so unkind we'd never have sent you off to them.'

'They weren't unkind,' Tom said. 'It wasn't that. I can't explain. I don't want to talk about it.'

Just thinking about the Norrises made him feel sad and guilty.

'OK,' Simon said. 'Don't worry. You're home again and no harm's done. That's the main thing.'

The official had been standing back, but now he edged forward again.

'They're waiting for you now, if you can come with me,' he said.

'Who's waiting?' said Tom. He felt as if a weight had rolled off him and he was kilos lighter. He almost wanted to walk on tiptoe. 'Are Afra and Joseph here?'

Simon and Debbie exchanged astonished looks.

'No,' said Simon. 'Didn't you know, Tom? About the press being onto you and everything?'

'The press?' Tom looked worried. 'No.'

'Well,' said Debbie, and a look of excitement replaced the fond anxiety in her face. 'The newspapers and TV and everyone have heard the story about what you did on the way over to England. Of course, I knew they must be exaggerating. You only gave information about some suspicious person, didn't you? I don't believe for a minute that anyone could possibly have been actually smuggling live animals onto an aeroplane!'

'I know.' Tom nodded. 'I couldn't believe it myself at first.'

She stared at him.

'You mean it's all true? Next you'll be telling me you really did witness a smuggling transaction at the airport, and follow a criminal off the plane and chase him through customs?'

'Well,' said Tom modestly. 'Jas helped a bit.'

Simon let out a guffaw.

'I told you, Debbie. He's up to anything, our Tom is. They must have been having us on about you getting into a stranger's car, though. You didn't really do that, did you, Tom? Jump into the back of a criminal's car and let him drive off with you?'

Tom eyed his parents warily.

'I reckoned I knew where he was going, or I wouldn't have done it, honestly, Dad.'

Luckily, Simon seemed more amused than anything else. Tom started to breathe more easily.

'You'll be telling us next that all that stuff about black mambas and waistcoats full of vultures' eggs was true as well.' Simon laughed incredulously, like someone being told a good tall story, who wants to relish all the fictional details.

'There were eagles' eggs as well,' said Tom eagerly, 'only Rob, he's the guy at the Animal Reception Centre, he wasn't sure if they were Martial or Bateleur.'

He was aware that his parents were staring at him, bereft of speech.

'Yeah, and there was an iguana, and some Mantella tree frogs in the guy's camera bag,' he said, a bubble of happiness rising up in his chest, 'and a whole bunch of pancake tortoises. You wouldn't believe how they stop them moving, Mum. It's so cruel. They put a nail right in front of their noses, through the top and bottom shell.'

He was still talking when the official opened a door marked VIP SUITE. The flashes of a dozen cameras went off, almost blinding him, and voices started calling out from behind a battery of lights.

'Tom, how old are you?'

'Is it true that you rescued a fully grown vulture from someone's hand luggage?'

'Tell us how you fended off the black mamba that attacked you.'

'How many smugglers did you catch, Tom? Was it five or six?'

'Did you injure yourself when you rugby-tackled them to the ground?'

'Tom, look this way, over here, into the camera! Yes, that's it. Smile, Tom!'

'What I don't understand,' said Afra that afternoon when Tom, free at last, had gone round next door to see his friends, 'is how the press people knew anything about it, and worked out you'd be on the plane.'

'I wondered about that,' said Tom, 'but the TV reporter told me what had happened. If you really want to know, he said I had star quality. Talked well to camera. Excellent interview techniques.'

He lay back luxuriously on the grass, allowing Stumpy to nuzzle his feet, and waited until Afra and Joseph had finished snorting and rolling their eyes in disgust.

'It was Rob who broke the story, actually,' he went on. 'You know, the friendly guy I told you about from the Animal Reception Centre. He sort of guessed I'd be on the flight last night.'

'I thought you had to get away in deadly secrecy, and creep about like a ghost, and hadn't told anybody?' Afra said, puzzled. She and Joseph had listened with open mouths to the whole of Tom's story and had made him tell bits of it again and again.

'No, I hadn't told him exactly,' said Tom, 'because when I saw him I hadn't worked out what I was going to do. But he'd given me the idea, sort of, of coming home on my own. I reckon he knew I'd do it. He's so brilliant, Rob is.

'The thing is, he's got a mate here in Nairobi. The vet at the airport. They did a course together once or something. Anyway, Rob reckoned it would be easier for me with Mum and Dad if, well, if there was a bit of a fuss when I came home. So he phoned the airlines to see if I was actually on a passenger list on a Nairobi flight, and when he found I was, he phoned his vet friend and told him the whole story, and the vet started ringing round the papers and the TV and everyone, and honestly, you should have seen it, all the flashbulbs going off, and the TV cameras and everything, and all these guys jumping up and down, and asking daft questions like what colour Sweatface's trousers were, and how many times I'd flown round the world on my own without my parents knowing.'

'But your mum and dad, they must have been so angry with you,' said Joseph.

'That's the amazing thing,' Tom said. 'I thought they'd go really, really crazy with me, but they seem to feel guilty more than anything else, about trying to send me to such a crummy school, and to live with those people.'

'Those Norrises sound horrible,' said Afra. 'I'd have hated them.'

'You wouldn't,' said Tom. 'That's the worst thing. They just weren't used to kids. They tried to be nice, but living with them would have been like living in a cage. I'd have freaked out totally in the end.'

'Hey, guess what.' Afra had suddenly caught sight of Kiksy, her bushbaby, peering at her with his great moon eyes from behind the branch of a tree. 'Kiksy's been behaving real strange these last few days, getting out at night and coming home exhausted in the morning. I reckon he's found a mate. Wouldn't it be great if we had a whole family of these little fluffy fellers around the place?'

Tom sat up and held out his hand to Kiksy, who took a flying leap and landed on his shoulder. As the furry little creature took hold of his ear in his sticky little hands and hooted softly into it, he felt peace return to him, a solid, good feeling, even better than happiness.

I'm home, he thought. And I know I'm here to stay.

'You can hardly believe,' said Jas, six weeks later, as she and Tom stood looking into the new section of aviary built alongside Sunny's in the Singh garden, 'that that's the same bird who was all tied up in that horrible bandage in Sweatface's bag.'

The parrot was sitting on the perch nearest to the wire mesh that divided his section from Sunny's. He was whistling coquettishly, turning his head from side to side to look, first at Jas and Tom, then at Sunny. Sunny, pretending not to notice, was taking a dignified interest in a stick he was holding in one claw while demolishing it with his beak.

'I can't believe that you actually managed to get him back here,' Tom said admiringly, watching as the parrot took off and swooped down to the ground to retrieve a watermelon seed.

'It was thanks to Rob,' said Jas. 'He sent an

e-mail to the KSPCA, and said if they made a formal request this little guy could be sent back to be cared for by the family of Jas. He didn't know my other name, so he just said Jas, and hoped they'd find me. He needn't have worried. Everyone knows me and Mum at KSPCA. Mum e-mailed straight back and said we'd love to have him.'

'He seems happy,' said Tom, watching as the parrot flew back up to his perch. 'Pity they didn't send them both.'

'They said the little one would get too stressed to do another long journey,' said Jas, 'but they'll find a good home for him in Britain.'

Tom watched as the parrot spread his beautiful tail feathers, the colour of fire, and fluttered on his perch. Bound up in his little box, his beak taped cruelly shut, the bird had been reduced to an object, a thing for sale, a mere commodity, waiting for a price tag. But here, now, as the afternoon sun shot bars of golden light through the thick green leaves of the tree that shaded his roomy aviary, the parrot had regained something of himself. He was turning gracefully, climbing the rope from which his perch was suspended, casting backward glances towards Sunny, showing himself off.

It was easy to imagine the life he'd once known, the sociable, boisterous life of his flock, the rivalries and affections, the preenings and peckings, the soaring flights and aerial acrobatics in the dense green world of the forest canopy so high above the ground. He would never have that life again, but here, with Sunny for a companion, in a spacious aviary in this calm, beautiful garden, with devoted humans to look after him, he'd be safe at least, and might, if such a thing could be wished for a parrot, be happy.

'What are you going to call him?' Tom asked Jas.

'I don't know. I can't think of anything.'

Tom had a flash of inspiration.

'I think you should call him Gulliver,' he said. 'You know, like in *Gulliver's Travels*, because he travelled all over the place, and was caught and tied up, but he got himself home again all safe and sound in the end.'

Elizabeth Laird
**Wild Things 6:**
**ZEBRA STORM**

The Grevy zebra is unmistakable. It is the most beautiful of its kind. But there are very few of them left in Africa.

Joseph, Afra and Tom are lucky to find a magnificent Grevy stallion at a remote water hole. But it is alone and wounded, and a prowling lion is on its trail. Joseph is especially determined to save it. Like the zebra, he's in a desperate state. He's just been reunited with a man he's hated all his life – his father. Scared and angry, he runs away into the bush – straight into the lion's hungry jaws . . .

# WILD THINGS titles
# available from Macmillan

The prices shown below are correct at the time of going to press.
However, Macmillan Publishers reserve the right to show new retail
prices on covers which may differ from those previously advertised.

---

ELIZABETH LAIRD

| | | |
|---|---|---|
| 1. Leopard Trail | 0 330 37148 7 | £2.99 |
| 2. Baboon Rock | 0 330 37149 5 | £2.99 |
| 3. Elephant Thunder | 0 330 37150 9 | £2.99 |
| 4. Rhino Fire | 0 330 37151 7 | £2.99 |
| 5. Red Wolf | 0 330 37152 5 | £2.99 |
| 6. Zebra Storm | 0 330 37153 3 | £2.99 |
| 7. Parrot Rescue | 0 330 39301 4 | £2.99 |

---

All Macmillan titles can be ordered at your local bookshop
or are available by post from:

**Book Service by Post
PO Box 29, Douglas, Isle of Man IM99 1BQ**

Credit cards accepted. For details:
Telephone: 01624 675137
Fax: 01624 670923
E-mail: bookshop@enterprise.net

**Free postage and packing in the UK.**
Overseas customers: add £1 per book (paperback)
and £3 per book (hardback).